WATERMELON

By

Kate Hanney

Published in 2012 by Applecore Books
www.applecorebooks.co.uk

Copyright Text © Kate Hanney

Copyright Cover Images © Michael Hanney

A CIP catalogue record for this title is available from
the British Library.

To my friend Sarah, for her time, insight and enthusiasm, and for listening to me go on about my book for hours, and hours, and hours ...

And to the staff and students who I work with. I couldn't have done it without your interest, encouragement, and at times, cuttingly honest feedback!

WATERMELON

The cops came into school to show us this film once. It was a thing they were doing to try and stop kids carrying guns and knives, and they showed us what it looks like in slow motion when a bullet's fired into different things; a glass of milk, an egg, a watermelon – stuff like that. According to them, the one that's most like a human is the watermelon. The bullet slices straight through it. Its skin splits open as the whole thing explodes, then the mashed up flesh and juice splatter out into a big, red, gushing mess. If you go to Google videos and search for 'bullet' and 'watermelon', you'll find it.

Well I didn't actually see the bullet go into him that day. By the time I'd forced my eyes open, his body was already slumped in Frankie's doorway. But then I had to look at him up close, and that's when I knew they were right; it was red, and it was gushing, and it was a mess.

Difference is though, watermelons don't look back.

ONE

Dead cool I was when I walked into that social worker's office. I mean I'd done it all before, hadn't I? Seen the faces, heard the words, sat through the meetings. It wasn't just a case of having the T-shirt; I'd got the jeans, the trainers, and even the free laptop – well, I did have, 'til I sold it.

So I slouched down in the chair and stared at Molly. 'Go on then, who are they?'

'Who?'

'Who d'you think?'

She took a sip of coffee and smiled at me. 'I assume you're referring to your new carers?'

Oh the sarcastic comments. They pinged round my brain so fast I couldn't decide which one to go for, but in the end I didn't need any of 'em; my expression said it all.

Molly smiled again, then she picked a pen up off her desk and rolled it between her fingers and thumb. 'Well, actually, Mikey, you're not going to be living with new foster carers this time.'

The smart comments vanished and I frowned. 'What d'you mean?'

'Well, as you know, there's always a shortage of carers, and at the moment there's no one who we feel can successfully meet your needs.'

What the hell was she on about? I mean there'd got to be somebody, somewhere; they weren't gonna leave me to sleep on her office floor, were they?

'So what then?' I asked.

'Holly House,' she said cheerfully. 'It's a care home in Chapel Cross. The staff there are lovely. You'll be well looked after and you'll be with other young people your own age; you can make lots of new friends.'

I laughed. 'Are you daft?'

Molly stopped smiling. 'There really is nowhere else,' she said.

I sat up straight then. 'What? You're tellin' me that in the whole of Sheffield there's no carers that have any space? Not even for a few days, 'til you can sort somethin' else out?'

She chewed the end of the pen before she answered. 'It's not exactly that we have no carers available at all, Mikey, it's just that with your … difficulties … it has to be a very knowledgeable and experienced placement. They have to be people who are prepared to work with you. And at present there just isn't anyone who can do that.'

'Difficulties?' I shouted, as I jumped to my feet. 'I wouldn't have any fuckin' difficulties if you lot did your jobs properly and found me somewhere decent to live.'

Molly wheeled her spinny-round chair backwards a bit. 'I understand exactly how you must be feeling,' she said calmly. 'But I can assure you we did everything possible to find you a new carer; there was just nowhere that was appropriate. Why don't you try and keep an open mind? Give Holly House a chance? You might really like it.'

I shook my head. Would she really like it? Getting dumped somewhere you've never been to before?

Having to share a bog and a shower and a fridge with a load of strangers? Everybody knowing you're only there because absolutely nobody else wants you? At least in foster care you can try and pretend things are a bit like normal; pretend you're a bit like all the other kids who've got a home and a family.

I shoved hard against the desk with both hands. It was lighter than I expected, and it jerked back quicker and further than I thought it would. The mug went flying; coffee spilled all over the place, and the papers, folders and pens and stuff all got soaked. Some of it must've gone on Molly as well, cos she sprung up like Zebedee as I turned away.

'Mikey! You need to calm down. We can't discuss your placement properly while you're behaving like this.'

'It dun't sound like there's much left to discuss, does it? It sounds like all the decisions have already been made. As usual!' I punched the wall next to the doorframe and thought my knuckles were gonna explode with the pain. But they didn't, and it didn't stop me doing it again either.

I had to put my other hand on the wall then to keep me steady, and I leaned forward until my forehead pressed against the cold glass in the door. Closing my eyes, I concentrated on the blackness.

'I know it might not always seem like it to you, but we do try our best to place young people in the most suitable accommodation.' Molly's voice was quiet and controlled again. She carried on talking, saying loads of other words, but I didn't listen. I made myself think

9

about the dark. Don't let any other thoughts in your head, nothing else, just the darkness in front of your eyes.

Gradually, my breathing got slower, and by the time I looked back round the coffee had been wiped up and Molly was re-arranging the stuff on her desk. There was a photo of a dog I hadn't noticed before. It was one of those little grey things with hair like a sheep. The basket it was curled up in was all soft and fleecy, and a gold disk dangled down from its bright red collar.

'What if I don't go?' I said.

'There's nowhere else, love, honestly. It's where you should be now, and if you're not there we have to report you missing to the police. They'll just pick you up and take you straight back.'

Slowly, I went over and slumped in the chair again, but I kept my head down so Molly couldn't see my face.

She knew she'd won then. She knew this was her chance to get rid of me as well, and she jumped at it. 'I wanted to drive you over there myself,' she said, picking the phone up quickly. 'But something urgent came up so I ordered you a taxi. It should be here by now; I'll just phone down to reception and check.'

***

The taxi had come, and after half an hour of me pissing the driver off by fastening and unfastening the seatbelt, it pulled up at the bottom of some steps outside a tall, dark, terraced house in Chapel Cross. There was no sign or anything saying what it was, just a green front door that had a wooden board up where the glass bit should've been.

The taxi driver was supposed to wait 'til somebody came to meet me, but he didn't. 'There you go then,' he said, and he started writing something down in his book.

My trainers crunched on a load of shattered glass as I stepped out of the car and looked around. Most of the houses had those metal shutter things up to their windows and doors, and they were all covered in tags: *S16 ... Steely ... CCT Crew.* The edge of the road was lined with old chip papers and scratch cards and stuff, and somebody'd used the plastic seat under the bus shelter to wipe the dog shit off their shoes. Even the houses that were lived in looked scruffy. The gardens were overgrown, some of the windows were cracked, and although it was the middle of the afternoon, they all had their curtains shut tight.

Jesus, what're they playing at? Why would anybody put a kids' care home here? In one of the roughest parts of the city?

I suppose it's because all the people who live in nice houses, and who don't keep old mattresses and tellies in their front gardens, don't want a load of lager drinking, weed smoking 'youfs' hanging around on their street corner. And maybe you can't blame 'em. But whether they like it or not, they shouldn't have a choice. I mean I didn't have a choice, did I?

Reaching into my pocket, I pulled my last fag out and lit it quickly, then I watched as a little kid came wobbling down one of the paths opposite. All she had on was a baggy grey T-shirt that probably used to be white. She didn't even have any shoes on or anything, and she was just about to toddle through the glass on the pavement when a guy appeared. 'Atlanta, get back in this fuckin' house, now,' he yelled. The little girl stopped and looked at him, but she didn't move, even when he shouted, 'Now!' about another four times. Eventually, he stormed over to where she was standing, lifted her up by her wrist and carted her back into the house. She didn't make a sound the whole time.

The taxi drove off then, and I almost ran after it. I knew there was nowhere else for me to go, and I knew he wouldn't have let me get back in anyway, but I just didn't want him to leave me. Not here, not in this dump full of shit and scrubbers.

I took a long last drag on the cigarette and ground the butt into the pavement. I'd have gone absolutely anywhere with anybody at that minute, I know I would. If Hannibal Lecter'd turned up on his way home from the off-licence and invited me back for tea, I'd have been off.

But the sound of the door swinging open at the top of the steps, made me stop, and turn round.

TWO

'You must be Mikey?' An oldish, blondish woman stood looking at me. 'Come on in, we're expecting you.'

I glanced down the street again. The taxi'd gone out of sight, and there was no sign of Hannibal Lecter.

'Come on.' She sounded like she was talking to a five year old. 'You'll get cold standing there with no coat on.'

She wrapped her arms round herself and pretended to shiver. Then, cos I still hadn't moved, she came down the steps. She smiled and picked my bag up, and when she set off back towards the house, I found myself going after her.

'My name's Ruth,' she said, shutting the front door behind us. 'I'm your key worker, so anything you need or anything you're worried about, you just come and talk to me.'

She pointed to a door on the left. 'That's the lounge – there's a telly in there.'

There was also a hole the size of a football near the bottom of that door, and the daylight was shining through. Somebody must've given it a right kicking – probably the same person who'd smashed the glass at the front. There were two more rooms that she called the office and the dining room, then she said, 'And this's the kitchen.'

I followed her to the end of the hall and she pushed a door open. She went through it, but I stopped in the doorway   there was a kid in there. He had his foot up on one of the chairs while he tied his lace, then he looked at us.

'Oh, Shane, you off out?' Ruth said.

'Yep.'

'Where to?'

'Dunno.'

'Are you coming back for tea?'

'Dunno.'

'Well *please* get yourself home earlier than you did last night.'

'It weren't even that late.'

She tutted. 'It was late enough for us to report you missing – again. If you're not careful, you'll be getting another visit from the police.'

He grinned but stayed quiet. She stared at him, looked a bit pissed off, then sighed and carried on, 'Anyway, this is Mikey who's going to be staying with us.'

The kid half nodded at me. 'Safe, mate,' he said. Then he pulled his hood up to hide his dark brown hair and even darker brown eyes, and disappeared out of the backdoor.

Ruth slid the chair under the table. 'One of the rules,' she said. 'If you're not home by eleven o'clock each night, we have to report you missing to the police – so it's always a good idea to make sure you're in on time. Now, would you like me to show you your room?'

She either didn't care or didn't notice that I never answered her, she just wandered off back along the hallway, started going up the stairs and shouted, 'Come on, keep up.'

We stopped on the first landing we got to, but the stairs carried on upwards to another floor above. 'Bathroom,' Ruth said as she nodded at a room on the right. Then she unlocked the next door along. 'And this one is yours.'

Christ, I'd seen bigger cardboard boxes. There was a single bed that dipped down in the middle, a cream coloured wardrobe in the corner, and sod-all room for anything else. The carpet was dark red, which meant the stains were harder to see, but you could still tell they were there. It was pretty much what I imagined a prison cell to be like, except there were no bars at the window, and Ruth handed over the key.

'It'll seem more like home when you get your own things in it,' she said.

I glanced round it again. This was never gonna be my home.

'Anyway,' she went on. 'I'll leave you to unpack, then come down and we'll have a coffee and a chat.'

My stuff was in a black plastic bin liner – the last lot of carers had spent most of the money they got for me on themselves – so it didn't take long to put a few clothes, a can of Lynx and a toothbrush away. But when I'd done, I decided to hang around in the room for a bit; coffee gave me gut ache, and the last thing I felt like was a chat.

I went over to the window and looked down. It's where I was born apparently, Chapel Cross. For all I knew, I could've lived in one of the houses on this road. But I wasn't there long. Before I was even a year old, the social workers decided I was at, 'significant risk of coming to serious harm due to persistent neglect and suspicion of physical abuse.' My mum was, 'reluctant to engage with the support strategies that were being offered, and refusing to attend the parenting courses that were a fundamental requirement of the child protection plan.' I read the report, so I know.

And what all the posh words meant, what it also said in the report, is that my mum used to leave me in the house all night on my own. She forgot to change my nappy, and sometimes she didn't feed me. They started to notice bruises, and eventually, I ended up in hospital.

I don't remember foster carers one, two, three and four. Five were OK though; they kept me for ten whole years. They took me on holidays and made sure I went to school and stuff like that. But then she died and he couldn't cope with looking after me on his own, so I had to go back.

Six and seven lasted for about a month each, then 'carers' number eight were complete losers. Right from the beginning we hated each other, but they put up with me for nearly a year cos of the hundreds of pounds a week they got paid. I played up a lot while I was with them, and obviously, it's because of what they told Social Services when they sent me back, that nobody else would have me.

I sat down on the bed then and it made a strange sort of squelching noise. I folded back the duvet and the sheet, and saw a plastic cover stretched over the mattress. Jesus, I was fifteen years old, not fifteen months; what were they expecting? And apart from that, what kind of people had slept in, and probably pissed in that bed before me?

I scrambled off it as Ruth knocked on my door. 'Are you coming down for tea?' she asked. 'The others are dying to meet you.'

Great, that's just what I needed. But I bit the inside of my lip and turned to follow her.

'This is Mikey,' Ruth said, as we walked into the lounge downstairs.

There were four other kids in the home and they all stared at me. One was a lad who was about twelve. He dropped his eyes as soon as I looked at him and he didn't say a word. In fact, the whole time I was there I never heard that kid talk. Then there were two girls who were twins. They were older than me, probably about seventeen. They were all teeth and make-up, and between 'em they'd got more jewellery than Argos. The other one was Shane, the kid I'd seen earlier. He was standing next to the window shifting his weight from one foot to the other.

The girls nodded a bit, said hi, then looked at each other and burst out laughing. My face got hot, and obviously I felt like a right idiot. If I'd have known 'em better I would've given 'em a gobful, but you've got to be careful with strangers, haven't you? You never know who they are, or who they're related to, or who they might know.

Shane knew 'em though. 'Shut your faces, you gormy slags,' he said. Then he looked at me and flicked his head towards the door. 'Come on, mate, don't take any notice of them; they're a right couple of freaks.'

Ruth glanced from Shane to me. She shook her head a bit and I hesitated – what was she getting at?

But the lasses' voices screeched like sirens then as they yelled abuse back at Shane. Ruth tried to shout over 'em, telling us all how we should 'treat each other with respect' and 'speak to others appropriately,' and the quiet kid closed his eyes, covered his ears with his hands and started rocking backwards and forwards.

It was like a bleedin' mad house. I couldn't have cared less what Ruth'd been getting at anymore; I was outa there.

I took a big breath in as we jumped down the steps and landed on the pavement – the air wasn't exactly fresh, but it was better – then Shane took me round to Frankie's, a take-away on the next road.

'Burger an' chips, mate?' he said.

'Yeah, cheers,' I answered.

A few minutes later he passed me one of the polystyrene boxes, then he got a wad of tenners out of his coat pocket that nearly made my eyes pop – there must've been two or three hundred quid there at least. I looked away; he obviously hadn't got that through saving up his pocket money, and I decided it was best to pretend I hadn't seen it.

After we'd eaten our tea sitting on a wall, Shane rolled a spliff and shared it with me.

'You been at Holly House long?' I asked him.

'Two an' half years,' he said. 'Where you been before?'

'Foster carers.'

'I lived with some foster carers when I was little.

I've been in kids' homes since I was about ten though; carers never knew what to do with me when I kicked off. So how come you've ended up here then?'

'Last placement were a nightmare,' I said. 'They got the face on every two minutes, kept saying I was out of control. They even got a psychologist to prescribe me some medication.'

'Yeah? Did ya take it?'

'Nah, I gave it to their cat instead.' I smiled. 'Sixty mils of Ritalin a day I was givin' it; it were more chilled than a prawn at Iceland.'

Shane laughed, then he took a long drag and said, 'D'ya ever see your mum?'

'No. You?'

'No.'

It was silent for quite a while then, until Shane took a couple of Mars Bars out of his pocket. 'D'ya want one?'

'Nah; I'm full, thanks.'

He threw one over. 'Have it anyway, you can always save it for later.'

I held the end of the wrapper and swung the chocolate bar gently. He'd shared more stuff with me in the last hour than anybody else'd done in the last year. I wondered if I'd get chance to hang out with him again.

'D'you still go to school?' I asked. I could tell he was older than me, but I wasn't sure by how much, and changing schools again was one of the things I was dreading most; it'd be wicked to have somebody I knew there.

'I should go to Deep Brook,' he answered. 'They've

excluded me a few times, but they still said I could go back for the last few months before I leave. But I never go; I can't be arsed.'

'You don't just hang around at the home all day though, do you? I mean it'd do your head in.'

'Oh, I'm busy enough,' he said.

I stared down as bits of a torn up Euromillions ticket blew around my feet. Yeah, I suppose it would keep you busy: late nights, visits from the police, having all that cash to count. I dared myself to ask him about it, and I almost built up to it as well, but then this kid came round the corner.

'Hey,' said Shane, smiling, and he got up and went over to the lad.

They talked for a few seconds, then Shane turned towards me and said, 'Mikey, this is Rocco.'

'Alright?' I said.

Rocco completely ignored me, frowned, then looked back at Shane.

'It's OK,' Shane said. 'Mikey's safe.'

Slowly, Rocco's frown turned to a grin and he nodded at me. He was a big lad Rocco; like proper solid. He was only a year or two older than Shane, but he must've been well over six foot tall, and his arms were like Popeye's just after he's eaten his spinach.

Shane's mobile rang then, and he got a shiny iPhone out that was so new it still had some of the plastic cover on. He stared at the ground as he answered it, had a five second conversation, then said quietly to Rocco, 'Donny wants us.'

Shane looked at me. 'We've gotta chip, mate,' he

said. 'See ya later?'

'Yeah, later,' I nodded, and they walked off.

After drinking what was left of the Coke from my can, I took my own phone out of my pocket. The silver colour had flaked off the buttons, and the cracks in the screen had been there for ages. But it still told me I'd got no messages or missed calls, and no matter how long I looked at it, that didn't change.

By the time I put my phone back it was starting to get dark. A load of kids were coming down the road towards the shops, and I decided I oughta get out of their way.

So, with nowhere else to go, I stood up and headed back to Holly House on my own.

THREE

Even though I felt proper knackered, drifting off to dreamland in that little room with its bare walls and squelchy mattress was never going to happen. I stood at the window for a bit and watched a young guy pick tab-ends up off the street, then an old guy in a Picasso pick a lass up off the street.

But when they'd gone, I looked round for something else to do, and the Mars Bar Shane'd given me earlier caught my eye. Ten seconds later, the screwed up wrapper was in my hand and the Mars Bar in my gob. After I'd swallowed the last bit though, my teeth felt like they were stuck together with Super Glue, which was one more thing to keep me awake. So I found my toothbrush and went out to the bathroom.

At first, I couldn't get the water to run cold enough, and I'd been in there a bit when I heard footsteps banging up the stairs. I unlocked the door and saw Shane on the landing. A big red mark glowed on his cheekbone, but he smiled at me, put his finger to his lips, then went inside his room.

Before he'd even closed the door, one of the workers chased upstairs after him. 'Shane,' she shouted, marching past me like I wasn't there. 'Shane, open your door, now.'

'What?' His voice sounded quiet through the wood.

'Open your door.'

'Why?'

'I want to see you.'

'Go an' have a look in my file – there's a photo in

22

there.'

She put her hand on her hip. 'Shane, I am not messing around; open this door at once or I'll go and get the other staff to help me.'

Gradually, the door opened and Shane stepped out. 'Go on then,' he said.

She leaned over to one side, pulled his hood back slightly and examined his face. 'How did you do that?'

He shrugged.

'Oh, come on, Shane; it's the size of an orange – you must know how you did it.'

'I fell.'

'Where?'

He glanced around. 'There,' he said, smiling. 'At the top of the stairs, just now. I tripped on the top step and went flying into that doorframe.' He looked at me. 'You saw it, Mikey, din't ya?'

Both sets of eyes burrowed into me then. But I never even hesitated; she couldn't have meant much less to me, him liking me couldn't have meant much more. 'Yeah.' I nodded. 'That's exactly how it happened.'

The worker pulled a face like she'd bit into a jalapeno as she turned back to Shane. 'So what was all that about then, keeping your head down and hiding your cheek when I let you in?'

'Nowt; I don't know what ya mean.'

She made a sort of snorting noise. 'I think you know exactly what I mean.' Her other hand went on her other hip. 'Are you seriously expecting me to record it in the book as a fall?'

Shane shook his head and yawned. 'Record it as

whatever ya want.' He turned away and went in his room again.

The woman scowled at me for a second, then the stairs creaked as she waddled back down. I stood there; was that how it worked then? He lied, I lied, she knew we lied, and nothing much happened? Cool.

I ran my tongue over my teeth and decided they felt just about clean enough, but as I stepped over to my own room, Shane reappeared. 'Ta,' he said, leaning against the doorframe. 'It stops 'em askin' loads of questions if ya can convince 'em it were an accident.'

'Oh – I'm guessing it weren't then?'

He smiled. 'Nah, not unless ya call gettin' jumped by three tossers on a dark gennel accidental.'

'Really?'

'Yeah, really – believe me though, they went home with a lot more than a sore cheek.' He sniggered softly. 'They thought I were on my own, see, but I weren't … you should've seen their faces …'

He carried on laughing as he nodded at me and shut his door. I smiled, half wishing I had been there to see their faces. But as I walked into my room and looked at the tiny space, the dodgy bed and the minging carpet, that smile vanished quicker than a pie at a Weight Watchers' meeting.

***

When I went downstairs the following morning, Ruth was nowhere to be found, and I wasn't sure what to do; you know, about having a shower and getting some breakfast and stuff?

A guy with brown hair and a ginger beard was sitting in the office with the phone to his ear. I stood just outside looking in, and I could tell from the way he tried to act like he hadn't seen me, that actually, he had.

After watching him ignore me for a few seconds, I gave up and went and peered round the door into the lounge. The quiet kid was sitting on the floor with a load of these little toy figure things round him – I think they were like warriors or something. As soon as he saw me though, he scooped 'em all up in his arms and started rocking again. I think he must've stopped breathing as well, cos his lips started to go blue.

I backed out quickly, and wondered if I oughta tell the guy in the office about his lips. But just as I was standing there deciding, Shane's voice came from behind me.

'It's alright,' he said. 'He always does it.'

'Does he?'

'Yeah, he'll stop in a minute if ya leave him alone.'

'I wasn't … '

'No, I know ya weren't, mate. He just gets like it sometimes, 'specially if he dun't know ya.'

'Oh.'

'Me an' Rocco are goin' into town for a bit,' he said then. 'You wanna come?'

My face went from gobsmacked that he'd invited me, to buzzin' at the thought of getting out of that house and not being on my own, then to gutted because I didn't have any money.

'Have they give ya your allowance yet?' Shane

asked.

How'd he guessed what I was thinking? I looked at him and shook my head.

'Tight bastards.' He took a ten pound note out of his pocket. 'Here, take this; it'll put you on for a bit.'

I gawped at the money, then him. 'I can't … I mean cheers and all that, but I don't know when I'll be able to pay you back.'

'Don't worry about it. I owe ya one for last night, don't I?' He moved his hand nearer and I slowly reached out and took hold of the money.

'C'mon then,' he said, leading the way towards the door. And I scrunched the note up in my hand as I tagged along after him.

We went into Currys first. The new laptops and iPads and stuff were wicked. Me and Rocco messed about on 'em for ages, but Shane soon got side-tracked when one of the lasses who worked there came and asked him if he wanted any help. I've no idea what they talked about, but from the way she giggled and fluttered her eyes, I guessed it wasn't the current state of the electronics market. After about ten minutes, the manager stropped over and told her she had to serve somebody else, but she was still watching Shane as we left, and he flashed her a massive smile.

'She were alright,' Rocco said to him. 'You get her number?'

'Yeah, course I did.'

'What's her name?'

'Err, Casey ... or Keely; summat like that.'

'You gonna call her?'

'Dunno, depends.'

'What about that lass from Previews; you still seein' her?'

'Nah – she started gettin' all serious, wouldn't leave me alone.'

'Christ.' Rocco sniffed. 'I wish somebody like her'd get serious about me. I'm tellin' ya, ya definitely should have stayed with that one.'

Shane smiled. 'Like that's ever gonna happen. There's no point gettin' stuck with one bird when the whole sky's full of 'em, is there?'

Rocco thought about it 'til we turned to go into CJ's, one of the best designer shops in the city. Two kids were just on their way out though, and when Shane and Rocco saw 'em, and they saw us, everybody stopped. None of 'em said a word; they just stood there staring at each other. They weren't right tall the other kids, but they were as wide as busses. I moved in a bit closer behind Shane and Rocco.

'Excuse me.' A woman pushing a pram opened CJ's door to get out, and she stood waiting for us to move. Rocco stepped back first, but he still never took his eyes off the two kids.

Shane didn't move at all, so they had to squeeze past him to get out of the doorway. They turned back once they had, but the woman was still between us, struggling to get the pram down the step. A few seconds later, they walked off.

'Who were they?' I asked Shane, once the woman had gone and we were inside the shop.

'They work for Kaler,' he said.

I glanced at him and shrugged.

'Kaler,' he went on. 'He runs S22; Northwood and all round there. They're a right load of retards, him and his boys, but they think they're like proper hard.'

'Yeah,' Rocco said, holding a pair of jeans up. 'And we still owe 'em for what they did to Jake. They were lucky that woman come along, or I'd have battered 'em.' He reached into his pocket and took some money out. 'I'm gonna have these,' he said, and he went off towards the back of the shop.

Some kids are always threatening to batter other kids, aren't they? They go on about it all the time. But I could tell, as I watched Rocco paying for his jeans, that he really meant it. If that woman hadn't have come between us, it would've all kicked off.

'What d'ya think of this?' Shane had a dark blue Boss hoodie in his hand.

'Yeah, I like it,' I said.

He looked at it again, then went and bought it.

So when we all walked out of the shop, I was the only one who wasn't holding a CJ's carrier bag. I felt at what was left of the tenner in my pocket. Oh well, at least I was there; at least I had somebody to hang out with.

We decided to go to McDonalds for dinner, and as we cut through some of the backstreets to get there, we went across this kind of bridge thing at the side of the market. Rocco stopped halfway along and looked at the alleyway underneath. 'Remember that time the cops chased us and we had to jump down there?' he said to Shane.

'Yeah.' Shane smiled. 'Ya can still see the crack in the concrete where your head hit it.'

'I know.' Rocco nodded. 'I ended up gettin' constipation.'

'Eh?' I frowned and smiled at the same time.

'Well, it's a bigger drop than you think,' he said, as he walked on across the bridge.

I still didn't get it, so I looked round at Shane. His shoulders were shaking and his whole face was laughing, even though he was trying hard not to make any noise. 'He means concussion,' he managed to say.

I couldn't help laughing out loud at first, and it took me right until we'd made our way over the bridge and down the road to McDonalds, to eventually shut up.

Three Big Macs and a couple of Bensons later, we were heading towards the arcades. I was thinking I ought to save the few quid I'd got left, but knowing I probably wouldn't, when Rocco nudged Shane and nodded at a lad on the other side of the road. 'That looks proper like Robbie, dun't it?' he said quietly. 'I mean obviously it's not, cos Donny made sure he din't walk or talk no more, but it looks right like him.'

Shane didn't even glance at the kid, he just stared at Rocco and shook his head. Rocco was baffled at first, but he looked at me, then back at Shane, and his expression turned into one that said, 'Ooops.'

'Why, what d'you mean? What happened?' I asked before I could stop myself.

'Oh it's nowt,' Shane said. 'Here, d'ya want another fag?'

He handed me a cigarette and I lit it. What were they

on about though? Who was this Donny guy? I had to know, cos there was somebody called Donny who I'd heard of, see. Kids talked about him in school yards all the time, some of 'em even claimed he was their uncle or cousin, or that their dad was his best mate – that was all a load of bollocks though; I'd never met anybody who really knew him before. But everybody made him out to be some kind of big shot gangster – you know, drugs, cars, guns … 'nuff respect'?

It'd sort of crossed my mind the night before, when on top of all the other stuff, Shane got that call. I mean obviously there was more than one guy called Donny around, but I couldn't help wondering if it was the same person. And now, after what Rocco'd just said, I was starting to think it was.

I looked at Shane and Rocco. Were they really mixed up in all that? I was dying to find out, but Shane'd made it clear he didn't want to tell me and I daren't push it. If they did hang out with Donny I'd be crazy to go upsetting 'em, and even if they didn't, it's not like I'd got so many friends that I could afford to go pissing any of 'em off.

The music from The Simpsons blasted out then, and Shane answered his mobile. 'How much d'ya want?' he asked the caller. Then after a few more seconds he said, 'Yeah, I can do that. I'll see ya behind Carter's – it'll be about an hour though.'

He hung up and smiled at us. 'Gotta go, boys,' he said, and he turned and disappeared into the Saturday shoppers.

Me and Rocco still went over to the arcade for a bit,

but it wasn't long before his phone rang and he had to leave as well.

So I was back to being Mikey-no-mates; wandering through town by myself. Except that now, every so often, my face broke into a smile – constipation, concussion – you couldn't have made it up, could you?

Shane and Rocco were definitely a cool couple of kids, and although I hated to admit it, maybe Molly'd been right? Maybe Holly House wasn't such a bad place after all? I mean like she said, I was starting to make new friends.

FOUR

Over the next three or four months, things worked out OK. Deep Brook wasn't that bad, so most of the time I went to school during the day, then me and Shane chilled out together afterwards. Usually we smoked a joint in the park or went into town for a bit. Rocco came with us as well sometimes and it was proper cool – but sooner or later there'd always be a phone call, and then they'd have to go.

Although they were sort of careful not to go into detail, they did talk more about Donny and dealing and stuff as they got to know me. A lot of what they got up to was well dodgy, I knew that, but it was up to them, right? They only did what loads of other kids did, and they were always proper safe with me – which basically, was all I cared about.

We never talked about it much, but I could tell a lot of the things that'd happened to me had happened to Shane as well, and he knew what it was like.

Also, Shane always had money in his pocket, and because he knew my allowance from the home didn't even keep me in fags, he paid for stuff all the time.

Most days he got us food from the takeaways so we didn't have to mess about making it ourselves, and sometimes, when I'd run out of credit on my phone or something like that, he gave me a few quid to put me on. I felt a bit awkward about it at all first, but he told me not to be daft and that he wouldn't do it if he couldn't afford it. So I took it.

The other thing Shane bought for me was cigarettes;

loads more cigarettes than I actually smoked. This meant I could sell the rest, and I started to make a bit of money of my own.

One day in the park, I told him how much the kids at school would pay for a fag when they were desperate. Shane looked at me and laughed.

'That's cool mate,' he said. 'But you know, if ya wanna earn some proper cash, I could probably sort it out for ya … if ya want me to?'

'I don't know,' I shrugged.

There were times when I really wanted to be like Shane; when I wanted to have what he'd got. Obviously the money was wicked; clothes, phones, booze, weed – he could buy whatever he wanted. But it wasn't just that, it was the friend thing as well. Shane was one of the boys; he belonged to something. The other lads were pleased to see him when they met him on the street, and if one of 'em was in trouble, it'd only take a phone call and they'd all be there.

Rocco was the one I knew best, but there were others as well: a kid called Paulie, Paulie's younger brother, Jake, three or four others whose names I didn't know. And they all looked out for each other.

But I wasn't stupid either. I knew Shane and the others worked hard for the cash they got. There was always the chance they'd get picked up by the cops, and if they did, there was the chance they'd get banged up for a long time. Donny kept a pretty close eye on 'em as well, and if he asked 'em to do something, they did it; no questions asked.

Then there were the other gangs. I mean I'd found

out Donny looked after the whole of S16, which included Chapel Cross, but there was still trouble sometimes. The Kalers and Donny's boys had some proper bust-ups every so often, which usually ended up with at least one of 'em getting hurt bad.

But the thing that was really on my mind, was my mum. After talking to Ruth a few weeks back, I decided to send her a letter – maybe people do change? So I wrote and asked her if she was OK, I told her a bit about myself and said I'd love to see her. I even said I missed her. The social worker promised to deliver it, and I was still waiting to see if my mum replied. If she did, and if I did get to meet her, I thought it'd be better if I could show her that I was going to school and doing well and behaving myself.

I shook my head a bit. 'I don't know,' I said again.

I could tell Shane had a good idea what'd been going through my mind for the last couple of minutes, and he smiled.

'It's cool,' he said. 'Just let me know if you change your mind.'

***

It's amazing how quickly you do change your mind sometimes, isn't it?

A few days later I was in the school yard at dinnertime. I was selling a few fags and having a smoke myself when a lad called Simon came up to me. I didn't like Simon, he was always acting clever and he thought he was ten men. We'd had a few run-ins since I'd been there.

'Let's have one,' he said, with a greasy smirk on his face.

'You still owe me for two you had last week,' I answered. Normally I didn't mind giving a few away here and there, but this was Simon, and I hated him.

He laughed. 'Oh come on, you and your bum boy mates down at that home have got tons of 'em. It won't hurt you to share.'

Two kids standing next to me stopped talking and looked at us. I stared down at Simon's brand new Timberlands, then slowly moved my eyes up to his smug white face. 'Fuck you,' I said quietly.

He cocked his head to one side, pulled his shoulders back and bounced up to me. 'Who you talkin' to?' he yelled. 'Eh, I said who you talkin' to? Pussy. There's no wonder your mother didn't want you, you ugly retard. I bet she couldn't even stand to look at you. Or was it because she was too busy screwin' around that she had no time for you?'

I blinked once then glared at him. I knew the bit about me being ugly was a load of crap. I mean I don't want to show off, but one thing I do have going for me is my looks.

But what he said about my mum, that was too near to the truth. My heart started banging about in my chest and my head felt sort of tight. It was like I could actually hear the sound of blood rushing through my body.

A load more kids gathered round us. Simon looked at 'em, then began to bounce again. 'Well, I'll smash your ugly face in if you ever talk to me like that again. You got that?'

He'd been pointing at me as he'd shouted, and I reached up and pushed his hand away. 'Fuck you,' I said, just as quietly as before, and I stared right into his eyes.

Simon threw a punch, but as it turned out, he was the pussy and it hardly touched me. I grabbed his top, swung him round and pushed him up against the wall that'd been behind me. Then I proper laid into him. Blood splattered from his lips within a few seconds, and his head jerked one way then the other as my fists smashed into it. He almost bent double when I punched him in his stomach, and he started to slide down the wall. But my mind was still going crazy. I yanked him back up and belted him in his face again. If I'm honest, I probably would've carried on until … well, I don't know when. But my arms were gripped then, and two of the teachers dragged me away.

Even though Simon was struggling to stay on his feet, and the spit dribbling out of his mouth was a mixture of frothy white and bright red, I still pulled and twisted about all over the place trying to get back at him. His words rang in my ears like an alarm clock; *too busy screwin' around … no time for you.*

But some of the other staff helped Simon back into school then, and as I watched him shuffling away, I started to calm down. Not smirking much anymore, are you, clever bastard?

Eventually, they decided it was safe to let me go, and they took me to the Head Teacher's office.

'I'm very disappointed with your behaviour,' he said, shaking his head and looking … disappointed. 'You've done so well since you joined us; all of your teachers have commented on what an intelligent, articulate and polite young man you can be.'

'That's down to foster carers number five, sir,' I said.

He looked puzzled for a second then moved on. 'What on earth made you do such a thing?'

I told him what Simon had done and said.

'Well, I can understand why you might have felt angry,' he said. 'But surely it didn't warrant such an extreme response? The aggression and violence that you displayed is completely unacceptable. You should have told a member of staff and we would have dealt with it appropriately. I really don't have any other option but to issue you with a fixed term exclusion. I'll phone your carers and let them know you're on your way home.'

Tosser, I thought. And just before I got to the door, I turned back round and looked at him. 'Have you got any kids, sir?'

He hesitated, then said, 'Yes.'

'Do you love 'em?'

'Yes, of course I do.'

'There ain't anybody in the whole world who loves me,' I said.

Then I stood and watched him fidget and splutter and scratch around for something to say, before I walked out.

***

So, anyway, that's how I ended up hanging around the home all day, and I was so bored I could've cut my own fingers off just for something to do. As usual, Shane went out a lot, and for a while I managed not to even think about going with him. But then one morning, Ruth came to talk to me.

'Molly's been on the phone,' she said. 'It's not good news about your mum I'm afraid. They went round to see her and they took your letter, but she doesn't feel that she wants to have any contact with you at the moment. I'm sorry.'

I know I shouldn't have hoped for anything else, but deep down I had, and now it was hard.

'OK,' I said.

Ruth put her hand on my shoulder, but I shrugged it off.

'Do you want a drink or anything?' she asked.

'Nah, I just wanna be on my own for a bit.'

'Right, yes, of course. Well, just give me a shout if you want me.'

She got up to go, but I stopped her again. 'Did she read it, the letter?'

'Yes, love. She read it, but then she gave it back to them.'

She went and I sat staring at the telly. That was it then: no contact, no family.

I should've never bothered. If she had changed, and if she had started to care about me, then she would've tried to get in touch herself, wouldn't she? You see women all the time on these TV programmes, saying how a day never goes by without 'em thinking about the child they had to give up. How they miss 'em and would do anything to find 'em again.

Not my mum though. Stupid slag.

I could have been born to anybody, couldn't I? I mean like, you get conceived and then you're born. And it's nothing to do with you is it? You've got no control over who shagged who or whose belly you have to develop in. You just get born and you have to hope it's to somebody who wants you.

Lifting my foot up, I kicked out hard at the coffee table in front of me. At first, it just lifted up on to two legs then dropped back down again. So I jumped up and had another go. This time it flipped right over on to its side, and the loud crash it made as it hit the wooden floor sounded good. I glanced round; what next then? The telly, the pictures, the curtains? Maybe all of 'em?

But a familiar sound stopped me. Standing still, I listened as Shane's footsteps thudded down the stairs, along the hall then into the kitchen. Slowly, I turned away from everything else, and decided to go after him.

'Alright?' he said, just before he downed half a pint of milk in one go.

'Can I chill with you today?' I asked him.

He looked down into the bottom of his glass for a second, then as his eyes came up again, he said, 'You sure?'

'Yeah.'

Shane went into the other room to make a call, and when he came back in he said, 'Come on then, mate, I'll take ya round to see Donny.'

FIVE

It took us about ten minutes to walk up to the row of shops near the school playing fields, and for the first five of 'em, all I could think about was my mum. If I'd have known where she lived I'd have gone straight round there. I'd have told her what a shit mother she was, how much I hated her, and how I was better off without her anyway.

But as we got closer to the shops, my mind started to focus on Donny instead. What was he gonna be like? This guy I'd heard all those kids talk about? This guy who could make Shane drop whatever he was doing just by making a phone call? This guy who'd made sure some kid never walked or talked anymore?

My footsteps slowed down, and Shane stopped and looked at me. 'What's up?' he said.

'That kid, that one you an' Rocco talked about once – Robbie. What happened to him?'

Shane shook his head a bit. 'It's nowt. You don't need to bother about it.'

I knew I probably should've left it. But I couldn't; so I took a chance.

'Go on,' I said, trying to smile. 'Tell me.'

Shane sighed. 'It's not even that excitin'.' But he glanced quickly up and down the street, and decided to carry on. 'Robbie were a kid that used to work for Donny about two years back. But he got clever, right, an' he started skimmin' off the top. Donny found out, an' him an' a couple of the boys went round to Robbie's house. Nobody really knows what happened there, but Robbie weren't ever seen again, an' accordin' to the neighbours, the council had to paint all the walls before anybody else could move in, cos they were all sprayed with blood.'

I stared at Shane. The inside of my lip'd already started to swell up cos I was biting it so hard.

He looked away for a second then shrugged. 'He were a dickhead, Mikey. He got greedy and tried takin' Donny for an idiot. None of the other boys've ever had any bother – if you're sound with him, he'll be sound with you. OK?'

I managed to nod.

Shane reached his hand out and patted the sleeve of my jacket. 'Cool,' he said, and after a bit of a pause, we walked on together.

Walls sprayed with blood. Can you imagine it? Cream coloured walls with splatters of red all over the place. Streaky dark lines where it'd run down. And what about the floors? They must've been covered.

Every step I took seemed to be getting harder than the one before. I mean, what must they've done to him to make his blood splatter like that? They must've –

'You seen Rocco's new car?' Shane's voice was exactly like normal.

'Err, no – I din't even know he'd got one.'

'Yeah, it's alright. One of them new Hondas; only about a year old. Donny got it cheap for him off one of his mates, he lent Rocco the money an' all; says he can pay him back whenever.'

I watched Shane for a bit, and I could tell he honestly believed Donny was OK. He knew all about

41

the Robbie thing – and probably about loads more other things as well – and yet he still hung out with him. That'd got to mean something, right? I mean Shane wasn't daft; he knew the score better than anybody. And, also, he was my best mate; there's no way he'd be taking me to see Donny if he didn't think he was safe.

Maybe what he'd told me wasn't even true – you know, about the blood and that? It was only what somebody'd said, Shane didn't know it for sure. Perhaps Donny'd just scared that Robbie off? He'd been bang out of order, hadn't he? You couldn't expect Donny to just sit back and let him get away with it. And, like Shane'd said, it was nothing for me to be bothered about anyway, cos I'd never do anything like that; *sound with him, sound with me.*

We'd passed an off-license, a barber's, and every different kind of takeaway you could think of by then, and Shane stopped outside this café. 'This's it,' he said. 'You alright?'

'Yeah … sound,' I said, and we both smiled.

The woman behind the counter didn't even look up from the frying pan as we walked in and went straight through to the back. There was a corridor in front of us with three doors off it, and Shane knocked softly on one of 'em. My mouth felt as dry as stale bread, and my breakfast swirled around inside me.

Slowly, Shane pushed the door open and moved to one side so I went in first.

The room was a lot smaller than I'd expected. A massive flat screen telly almost filled the wall in front of me, and some thick curtains completely covered the wall to my left. I suppose there must've been a window behind the curtains, but I couldn't be sure because no light got through at all from the outside. On the other wall, there was a solid wood door that must've led out to the back of the café.

Donny'd been laying back in one of those leather chairs that recline, but he sat up straight as we went in.

He was probably about thirty, and I'd never seen anybody with black hair have such pale blue eyes before, but he had. His clothes were all Armani and his trainers, Y3s. When he opened his mouth into something a bit like a smile, his teeth were gleaming white. But then the door closed behind us and it got darker. The room was just lit by the telly after that, and it meant I could only really see Donny as a silhouette.

'You're Mikey, right?'

Christ, his voice was so quiet you could hardly hear it. Was he ill or something? Or did he always talk like that?

I swallowed. 'Yeah,' I said.

'What's your full name?'

'Michael Hartson.'

He said something else then, but I had absolutely no idea what. I turned towards Shane, desperate for him to help me out. But he'd edged up right close to the telly, and although his hood covered most of his face, I could tell his eyes were fixed on the screen. Donny's leather chair creaked as he altered his position, and I looked back. He was leaning forward, smoothing a crease out near the bottom of his jeans, but once he was satisfied it was all sorted, he straightened back up and stared at me.

Sirens screeched on the telly, and a blue light flickered round the room. I took one last glance over at Shane, but he still hadn't budged. So all I could do was lean in a bit closer, wet my lips and say, 'Sorry, I didn't hear you.'

'I said, have you got any record with the cops?'

His words were still quiet, but thank God I managed to make 'em out that time. 'Oh, no. No I haven't.'

Donny tilted his head slightly to one side. 'You sure?'

'No – I mean, yeah – yeah, I'm sure.'

The insides of my stomach jumped into my chest. How could he make me feel like I was lying when I knew I wasn't?

His eyes moved up above mine then and after a pause, he nodded. 'How'd you get that?'

He meant the scar I've got above my right eye. It's a bit like the one that wizard kid in the films has got on his forehead, but I ended up with mine thanks to my mum's pimp and his flick knife.

'I've had it since I was a baby,' I said.

Donny kept on staring at the scar. I tried hard to work out what he was thinking, but there was absolutely no expression there at all; it was like being face to face with a great white shark. My fingers found the zip on my jacket, and slowly, I zipped it up right to the top. Music blasted out as the cop show on the telly went off, and I felt Shane finally starting to take some notice. I daren't look at him though, cos Donny still hadn't taken his eyes off me. All I wanted to do was pull my hood up and get buried inside it, but I made myself stand still.

Donny looked down then. He examined the back of his hand, before he put the tip of his thumb in his mouth, chewed off a tiny piece of nail, and spat it on to the floor.

Then he spoke again. 'Well, Shane tells me you're sound. He says you're a clever lad and you can keep quiet.'

I couldn't help smiling a bit, even though I tried not to show how buzzin' I was about what Shane'd said.

'That's good,' he went on. 'You'll be OK – I'll make sure you're OK – as long as you keep your head down, do what you're told, and stay quiet. You think you can do that, Mikey?'

'Yeah, sure.'

He stood up. 'OK. Hang around with Shane for a bit and we'll see how it goes.'

I watched then as Shane handed a load of notes over to Donny and told him what gear he'd got left. Donny counted out some different packets and wraps and passed 'em to Shane. Then they talked about some kids who'd owed Shane money for over a week. Donny told him to get hold of Rocco and that the three of us should go and see 'em. Then we left.

As we walked along, Shane tried to call somebody on his phone but they didn't answer.

'Idiots,' he said, shaking his head.

Then he called another number and spoke to Rocco. 'Alright? ... Yeah, meet us at Spots in about twenty minutes ... I got Mikey with me.'

'Spots?' I said, as he put his phone away.

'Top Spot,' he answered. 'That snooker club over on Bank Street. It's where these kids hang out that we've got to see.'

'What ya gonna do?' I asked him, feeling dumb, but really needing to know.

'Relax, man,' he said with a grin. 'We'll probably just end up talkin' to 'em. But they've gotta know we're gettin' impatient. They're takin' the piss and not answering my calls, so we just need to see 'em, that's all.'

Cool, I thought, we're just gonna talk to 'em, that's easy ... *probably* ...

When we got to the snooker club, Rocco was already waiting at the door. Shane went inside for a look round, but he soon came back out and told us they weren't there.

'We'll wait,' he said, and we crossed the road and went up a side-street opposite. We went far enough along so we couldn't be seen from the main road, but we could still see the entrance of the club.

We smoked a few fags and Shane and Rocco talked about what'd been happening with some of the other kids they knew. A couple of 'em worked for Donny, but most of 'em were with the other dealers. What I soon realised though, was that all the stories were more or less the same. They all began with things like, 'Did you know so and so got proper banged? ...' And, 'So and so's got fifteen years hasn't he? ...' And, 'Do you remember him what grassed so and so up? He got what were comin' to him ...'

After a bit there was a pause. I'd already started

thinking about it all, but then Rocco said, 'Hey, you know that big kid that works for Kaler? That one wi' dodgy eyes?'

Shane nodded, and Rocco carried on. 'Well, Paulie told me he got jumped by three kids from Ramworth last week, and he's in a right mess – missin' teeth, broken ribs – the lot. He said they smashed his knee into that many pieces, he had to have a metal plate put in to hold it all together.'

My teeth grated harder the more he went on.

'Wonder what he did to piss 'em off that bad?' Shane said.

'Dunno.' Rocco looked thoughtful. 'It's not like them boys always need a reason though, is it?'

'Nah, suppose not. It's like when …' Shane looked at me and shut up. He smiled, then got a tenner out of his inside pocket. 'You hungry?' he said, as he held it out to me.

I didn't answer, I just stared down at the money.

'Well we are. Go across to the chippy an' get us all some dinner will ya?'

Still without saying a word, I took the money off him and went, and by the time I was standing in the queue in the chippy a couple of minutes later, I was seriously thinking about not going back. I mean, I didn't have to do it, did I? I could just walk back to Holly House now; act like today'd never happened. I could still get out of it all …

But did I really want to go back? What was I going back to? What would Shane do if I did? And what would Donny do if I did? Jesus, my head started spinning like a waltzer.

'Yes, love?' The words came from the woman who was serving.

I stared across at her and blinked.

'What do you want?' she said louder.

Opening my hand, I stared down at the screwed up ten pound note. Well, it might all come at a price, but if I do end up getting my head kicked in, at least somebody'll care.

'Three chip butties,' I said, looking back at the woman, and after I'd paid her and covered the chips in salt and vinegar, I walked over to where Shane and Rocco were still waiting.

Shane changed the subject as I dished out the butties, and we started talking about which was the best chippy in Chapel Cross.

'Frankie's,' Rocco said, through a mouthful of mashed-up chips and bread a few minutes later.

'Nah,' said Shane, shaking his head. 'They're good for burgers and kebabs, but their chips are shit.'

'They're alright with curry sauce on 'em,' Rocco went on. 'And there's no wonder Frankie does the best curry sauce, is there?'

'Why, what d'ya mean?' asked Shane, looking confused.

'Well, he's Italian in't he?'

'Yeah, and …?'

Rocco tutted then spoke to us like we were thick. 'Curry? – Italy? – That's where all that kinda food comes from, innit?'

I nearly choked. Bits of my dinner spluttered out of

my mouth and all down my front. Shane burst out laughing as well. 'You goon. Curries aren't from Italy; they're from India.'

Rocco shrugged and carried on tucking into his buttie. 'Same thing though, innit?'

Me and Shane still couldn't stop laughing, and we daren't even look at each other for ages after that, because every time we did we started sniggering again.

I started to wonder how much longer they'd wait for those lads, but I didn't want to ask in case they thought I was getting bored. In the end though, we must've been there for about another half an hour, then Shane flicked his fag-end away and said, 'Here we are.'

Me and Rocco looked towards the snooker club as two figures disappeared inside, then all three of us made our way back across the road.

It was dark in the club and there were only a couple of tables being used. The bloke sitting behind the counter asked us if we all wanted to play, but Shane told him we just needed to have a word with some mates, and he pointed to the kids who were on the table furthest away. The bloke didn't look sure, but after thinking about it for a few seconds, he let us in.

'Don't say anythin',' Shane said quietly to me as we walked over to the far end of the club.

One of the kids saw us straight away; his face froze for a second, then he whispered something to his mate who was leaning over the table to take a shot. Without taking his eyes off us, his friend straightened up slowly, then they both stared at us in silence.

They were probably about eighteen or nineteen, but

they weren't big. I wondered if I should be bothered that they were standing there holding snooker cues, but as we got closer I noticed they were gripping them really tight, and their hands were shaking. That made me feel better.

'Alright?' Shane said.

'Yeah,' replied one of 'em carefully. He was speaking to Shane, but looking at Rocco.

'I've been callin' ya all week, but you never answered … how come?' Shane said.

Their eyes dropped and it was quiet for ages. They could have said all kinds of shit, like they'd lost their phones, or they'd never heard 'em ring, or they'd phoned him back and left a message and couldn't understand why he hadn't got it. But they knew they'd be stupid to lie, and telling the truth wouldn't have sounded too cool either, so in the end, neither of 'em answered.

After watching 'em for a minute, Shane spoke again, 'You got the cash then or what?'

Both kids looked at us, then at each other. One of 'em raised his eyebrows a bit, before he put his hand into his pocket and got his wallet. He held three twenty pound notes out to Shane, which was all he had, then he said quietly, 'Can we give you the rest tomorrow?'

Shane took the money and nodded. 'Yeah, here, tomorrow … four o'clock. Don't let us have to come lookin' for ya though, and don't keep us hangin' around either – we've wasted enough time on you as it is.' He paused for a second, then added, 'And it's not just me that gets pissed off when I'm owed money and my time's wasted, it's a lot of other people as well.'

Nobody said anything else, and we turned away.

I couldn't help grinning as we went back towards the home. I walked fast and felt sort of lively, like I had loads of energy. Those kids had been proper shitting themselves. Shane must be nearly two years younger than 'em, and I'm even younger than that. Rocco never said a word the whole time we were there, and none of us even laid a finger on 'em. And yet they were sweating like a fat bird.

That's respect, I thought – or is it fear? It didn't matter; I was buzzin'.

***

Ruth was just leaving when we walked into the kitchen at Holly House.

'Oh, I'm glad I caught you. Can I have a quick word?' she said. She glanced at Shane and added, 'In the other room?'

We went through into what's called the dining room. Nobody ever ate in it though, in fact it was only ever used for meetings, so it was always empty at that time of day.

Ruth smiled, then said, 'Molly phoned back just after you'd gone out this morning. She'd been writing up the visit to your mum, and she read through some files that had been archived ...'

I waited for her to carry on, but she didn't. 'So ...?'

'Well ... it seems ... it seems you've got an older brother, Mikey '

'What?' I couldn't take in what she'd said. I hadn't got a brother; I'd never had a brother.

'It's true.' Ruth nodded, but it was only when she kept on nodding that I started to let myself believe her.

'You sure?'

'Absolutely.'

I took a deep breath and laughed, and I just couldn't stop. A brother. Me. I'd got a big brother. Yes!

'What do you know about him?' I asked her eventually.

'Well, he'll be about twenty now. He went into care before you were born.'

'And where is he?'

'They aren't sure at the moment, but they can try and trace him – if that's what you want?'

'Course it is. What's his name?'

'Leon, Leon Hartson'

Leon, I thought, my brother, Leon. After all these years of thinking I had nobody … *after all these years*.

'So how come nobody ever told me about him before?' I said, not quite managing to sound stroppy.

'Well your mum had him before she moved to Sheffield. She'd been living in Leeds, and Leon entered the care system while she was still there. That meant that when your mum moved here, he remained under the care of Leeds local authority. All of his records stayed there.'

I got the feeling Ruth was trying to hide a cock-up at Social Services, but my head was buzzin' so much I didn't push it.

'So I'll tell them to go ahead and try to find him for

you, shall I?' Ruth said quickly.

I nodded.

She reached out and touched my arm. 'But you understand, don't you, there's a chance they might not be able to find him, and even if they do, he may not want any contact?'

I looked at her – I think after that morning I understood it more than anybody.

She smiled. 'OK, I'll get on to them tomorrow.'

Ruth left and I went up to my room. Don't get your hopes up, I told myself; anything could happen. But what I kept thinking, what I couldn't get out of my head, was that if he's twenty, he could become my carer. I could go and live with him.

Jesus, a lot could happen in a day, couldn't it? At eleven o'clock that morning I was completely on my own. Then suddenly, there's Shane and Rocco and Donny, and now Leon. I've got enough brothers to start my own five-a-side team.

SIX

The next afternoon, I was still wondering about Leon when Shane turned up with a new phone for me.

'Make sure you keep it charged up and switched on,' he said as he handed it over.

'Yeah, sure.'

He looked at me and his eyes got all sort of serious. 'I mean it, don't ever turn it off – not for any reason.'

I nodded. 'OK.'

He blinked and his eyes went back to normal, then he added, 'I've already put the boys' numbers in for ya.'

Holding the phone tight in my hand, I ran my thumb over the smooth screen and smiled.

I must've stood like that for a bit, cos the next thing I knew Shane was grinning at me. 'You can put it away ya know if ya want? It's not gonna ring straightaway.'

I laughed and shoved the phone in my pocket.

Then he said, 'A guy rang earlier, do ya wanna come with me to see him?'

'Yeah, OK.'

So we left Holly House and set off towards Greendale flats, which were in the middle of one of the estates nearby.

Normally, it would've taken a reinforced Hummer and an armed escort to get me into that area, even during the day. The kids who lived there never went out unless they'd got half their street with 'em, and it was a toss-up who was more scary; their Rottweilers or their girlfriends. I'm not kidding, if I'd have been on my own, they'd have had my new phone and I'd have had some new bruises within about five minutes.

But Shane wandered through the gangs of kids like they were pensioners at the seaside. They all knew who he was, see, and they all knew who he worked for.

Most of 'em just nodded as we walked past, but a few said alright to him, and they stopped to talk for a bit. Although none of 'em actually spoke to me, they all looked, and I could tell they were taking in who I was.

When we got to the car park round the back of the flats, a blue Fiesta was already waiting for us. There were two guys in it, and as me and Shane got nearer, one of 'em wound his window down.

'OK?' he said to Shane.

'Yeah,' Shane answered, as he leaned forward into the open window. 'Eighth?'

The guy nodded, holding twenty quid out in his hand.

Shane took the money, put it in his inside pocket, and brought out a small bag of bud.

'Safe,' the guy said, taking the bag.

And that was it. They drove off, and we went away from Greendale with twenty quid more than we'd gone there with. It wasn't all Shane's of course; most of it belonged to Donny. But Shane'd get his cut, and the more deals he did, the quicker all those cuts added up.

Rocco phoned to see where we were then, and he came over in his car to get us. Although I'd lived in S16 for quite a while, there were still parts of it I didn't know that well. So as we drove along, past the bookies and the Netto and the boarded-up convenience stores, they showed me all what counted as our area; the places where we were more or less safe.

We stopped to get a KFC after a bit and ate it sitting in the car. But before we'd even had time for a fag afterwards, their phones started to ring and we had to make a move.

By the time we got back to Chapel Cross it was getting late. We met the people who'd called, then went over to Previews, which was one of the busiest clubs round our way.

'I've no ID,' I said to Shane just before we got to the door.

He shook his head. 'You won't need any, an' you won't get searched either – Max an' Paddy are Donny's mates.'

I looked at him; *Max and Paddy?* He was winding me up, right?

Shane laughed. 'I'm tellin' ya, that's what they're called.'

I still didn't really believe him about their names, but everything else he said was true, and it was easier getting into that night club, than it would've been getting into the local youth club.

Inside, it was still fairly empty. Red and purple spotlights swirled around in the darkness, and the bass vibrated through my chest. I don't know what the floor was covered in, but it was like walking on toffee.

We went to stand at the bar, which was all lit up in red, and Rocco bought us a Coke. He must've seen the look on my face as he gave it me, cos he smiled. 'You've gotta keep a clear head, mate,' he said. Then he winked. 'Most o' time, anyway.'

Paulie and Jake, two of the other boys, came over and stood with us then. They were older than us, probably about twenty-two and nineteen, but to say they were brothers, they were nothing like each other. Usually, Paulie walked round like a Pitbull with a problem; I swear down, I've seen proper hard lads cross the street just to get out of his way. Jake though, laughed at anything. I mean don't get me wrong, he could turn it on when he needed to, but normally he was the kinda kid who'd find something funny about a fly crawling up a window.

Paulie got a drink, then said to Shane, 'What's he doin' here?' as he nodded at me.

'It's cool. Donny knows about him.'

'Jesus.' Paulie grunted. 'He'll be recruitin' 'em from bloody play group next. I hope this one can add up *and* keep his gob shut.'

He moved round, deliberately blocking me off from the others, and cos of the music I couldn't really hear what he said after that, but it suited me fine; it was better than having him glaring at me.

When they'd finished talking they split up, but I stuck close to Shane. The club was filling up fast by then, and as soon as he went and hung out in one of the dark corners, people started coming up to him. I watched how much they paid for stuff and listened to what they said; it was hardly advanced Brain Training though, trust me.

After a bit, I noticed Paulie crossing the dance floor and going up to a group of lads. He laughed and talked to 'em for a few minutes, then he handed out some gear. Instead of taking any money off 'em though, he just patted one of 'em on the back and turned away.

'What's he up to?' I said to Shane.

Shane glanced over at the lads. 'They're new in here,' he said. 'He's given 'em a few freebies, they think they've made a friend. But before they know it, he'll tell 'em they owe him. Then they'll have to find the money, and they'll probably keep on buyin' an' all. It's good business.'

I looked back over to where the lads were messing about and laughing. I hope you know where to get your hands on some cash quickly, I thought, 'cos you're gonna be needing it.

'Hi-ya!'

A lass's voice made me turn back. She was standing right close and smiling at me, so I suppose she must've been talking to me as well.

My eyes drifted from her long blonde hair, to her white lacy top, then down to her tiny denim skirt.

'Alright?' I nodded.

'You a mate o' Shane's?'

'Yeah,' I said, looking over to see him talking to another girl who must've appeared at the same time.

The blonde lass moved in even closer and put her arm through mine. 'So what's your name then?' she said.

'Mikey. What's yours?'

She told me, but I've no idea what she said. I was gonna ask her again, but she set off talking about something else, so I left it; I mean, knowing her name was hardly the main thing on my mind anyway.

Within about fifteen minutes, I'd found out that her lipstick tasted of cherry balsams and she had nothing else on under that top.

She clung to my hand like she'd clung to her Sambuca and orange as we pushed our way through the crowds to get to the door. I could see Shane still with the other lass, and I thought he was too busy to notice us at first, but a couple of seconds later he caught me up.

'Mikey,' he said, holding his hand out.

I could tell there was something in it, but I hadn't got a clue what 'til I reached out and took it.

I looked down and smirked. 'Cheers, mate,' I said, and I slipped the condom into my back pocket.

***

My bedroom was still spinning when I opened my eyes the next day; it'd been doing it when I'd gone to sleep as well. For a good hour, I didn't dare move in case I threw up; even breathing seemed a bit risky.

Eventually though, the boredom started to feel worse than my head, so I eased my way into the shower, blagged some Paracetamol off Ruth, then phoned Shane.

They were chillin' in a corner of the park, him and Rocco, and they both grinned when they saw me.

'Nar then, ya dirty stop-out,' Shane said as I sat on the grass next to him. 'Looks like you had a right party with Mucky Mandy?'

The memories from the night before made me smile, but I still felt proper sick, and the hot sun on my head wasn't helping.

'Did ya go back to her house?' Shane asked.

I nodded.

'Was her mum unconscious on the settee?'

I looked at him and nodded again.

'One empty vodka bottle and one just started?' Rocco asked.

'Oh, for Christ's sake,' I said, cringing.

Shane and Rocco nearly fell backwards laughing then. I couldn't help joining in a bit, but the thumping pain in my head soon made me stop, and for the tenth time that day, I asked myself why we'd had to finish *all* that vodka her mother'd left?

'What time did ya get back to the home?' Shane asked a minute later.

'About half three. You'd have thought I'd been missin' six months the way that new guy went on about it.'

'He's a right mardy bastard, in't he?' Shane pulled his cap down so it kept the sun out of his eyes. 'Maybe you oughta have an early night though, to make up for it?'

'What d'you mean? There's no way I'm gonna be in for eleven like they want.'

'Well I'm not sayin' it has to be that early, but you only get 'til twelve before they report ya missin' to the cops. Then ya might get some pain in the arse copper comin' round tryin' to find out where ya were. It's no big deal, but – '

'Shit.' Rocco stood up.

Me and Shane looked in the same direction as him, and saw two cops walking along the path from the kids' playground.

'Oh, shit,' Shane said quietly.

'What?' I knew cops were never good news, but it wasn't as if we were doing anything wrong.

'That big un.' Shane nodded. 'He's always lookin' for a reason to bust us.' He turned to Rocco. 'How much ya got on ya?'

'Enough.'

'Yeah, me an' all.'

'Shall we run for it?'

Before Shane could answer, the tallest cop looked up. He stared at us, said something to his mate, and their pace quickened.

Shane glanced at the high concrete fence behind us and the barbed wire that ran along the top. 'They're cornerin' us; we might not make it past.' His and Rocco's eyes searched about all over the place. 'There in't even nowhere to stash it.'

Panic started to show on their faces. The cops spread out more. What could I do? The last thing I wanted was to see 'em dragged off in handcuffs; they were my mates, we looked out for each other. 'I'll take it,' I said.

'What?' Both of 'em stared at me.

'I'll take it. If we split up, who they gonna follow?'

'Probably us.' Shane wiped his forehead with his hand. 'But, Mikey, you don't get it – if they search ya -'

'There's less chance of 'em searchin' me – you just said that. Quick they're nearly here.'

We huddled together and I took the little plastic bags off Rocco. Shane didn't move though.

'C'mon,' I said. 'It's OK.'

He sighed, but slowly handed over the bags. 'We'll try an' lead 'em away. If ya make it outa sight, hide it as soon as ya can.'

The cops were proper near by then. I kept my head down and we all set off in different directions. As they looked quickly between us though, one took a step towards me. Shit. What if we'd guessed it wrong? What if they did follow me? What if I did get caught?

'Stay where you are, lads; we want to talk to you.' The big cop's voice was proper strict. But I sensed Shane and Rocco start to run, so I did as well. We all dodged round 'em, and the cop shouted to his mate instead, 'You take that one.'

But I couldn't tell who he meant cos they were behind me by then. Our footsteps were silent on the soft grass and I had no idea if anybody was following me. I ran like mad, all the time hoping they'd gone after Shane and Rocco, and not me. The bags bounced about a bit in my pockets, and I put my hands on 'em so none fell out. This slowed me down though, and the sickly feeling in my stomach got even worse.

A second later, I got to the gate. I risked a quick look round, and blew out hard. Thank God; the only person near me was an old guy with a walking stick.

The cops'd just caught up with Shane and Rocco on the other side of the park, and by the way they'd slowed down it seemed like they'd let the cops catch 'em on purpose.

My breathing started to go back to normal as I went through the gate. All I had to do now, was hide it somewhere safe. I thought about it, then headed for a gennel I knew. The bushes around the entrance were all overgrown and these big thistle things lined the edges. Halfway along, some of the paving stones had broken. I lifted one up, dug a bit of a hole, then laid the bags underneath and stamped it back down. I didn't really want to leave in case somebody came and found it, so I hovered around until Shane phoned, and a few minutes later him and Rocco walked down the gennel.

'Are ya OK?' Shane still sounded out of breath, but he had a smile the size of a banana across his face.

'Yeah, sound. You?'

'We're cool. They searched us – some kids robbed Asda earlier, and *apparently,* we fitted the description – but they din't find nowt of course. Thanks to you.'

I looked away at one of the purple flowers on the waist-high thistles.

'I mean it, Mikey; that were like a right brave thing ya did.'

Rocco stepped forward. 'Yeah, and we'd have been in some proper shit if you hadn't.' He laughed and messed my hair up with his knuckles. 'You were like fuckin' Superman or summat.'

I laughed as well, but couldn't look at either of 'em properly cos my cheeks had got hot and I knew they'd be bright red as well, so I nodded at the broken paving stone instead. 'It's under there – is that alright?'

'Perfect,' Shane said. 'We'll leave it 'til we know they've moved on, then I'll get it in a bit. C'mon, let's walk up to the shop before I die of thirst.'

We made our way up the gennel together and the heat gradually disappeared from my face. It was a pretty big thing I'd done, wasn't it? And if I'd have thought about it more at the time, thought about what could've happened if the cops had caught up with me, I might not have done it at all. But God was I glad I had, cos it'd all worked out OK: my mates were safe, the bags were safe, and they really had treated me like some kind of superhero. A quick smile snuck its way on to my lips; was this what it felt like then, to be one of the boys?

***

It was two days after that when I made my first deal. Me and Shane went round to see Donny in the morning as normal, and after he'd sorted Shane out he looked across at me.

'You've done good so far, Mikey,' he said in his soft voice. 'The boys told me all about what you did in the park the other day; that was proper wicked.'

I wasn't right sure what to say, so I just smiled a bit.

'Here,' he said, counting out some bags. 'Why don't you have a go on your own?'

Slowly, I went over and picked 'em up. It was mostly weed, with the odd bag of charlie as well. For some reason, I started thinking about carers number five then. They were always right against drugs and stuff like that. I remember 'em telling me once about another kid they used to foster who ended up a proper crackhead, and about how he'd been a right lovely lad before he'd got hooked.

'You ready then mate?'

Shane was holding the door open. I looked at him then back at the bags. But it's not like it's proper hard stuff, I told myself, and if they don't get it from us they'll only get it from somebody else.

I pocketed the bags, and followed Shane out.

About an hour later, we were just finishing our hot roast pork sandwiches when Shane took a call. When he'd done he said, 'You wanna do this one?'

'Err, yeah – suppose so.'

'He's a sound enough guy,' Shane said. 'He's gonna be in a red Megane over in the car park at Greendale.'

Greendale? It had to be bloody Greendale, didn't it?

I drank my Coke, flattened the can with my foot and got up.

'Phone me if ya have any bother,' Shane said. 'And ya know how to get rid of it if there's any sign of the cops?'

'Yeah,' I said. 'I'll see you in a bit.'

While I walked along, I worked out what everything on me was worth all together. Then I did it again, cos I was sure I must've got it wrong – but I hadn't, and believe me, by the time I got to Greendale it wasn't just the sun that was making me sweat.

There must've been about ten kids standing on the first corner I had to get round. My back stiffened and I took my hands out of my pockets. Just keep on going, I thought; don't look at 'em but don't look away either, and don't walk too fast

As I got up to 'em though, they slowly spread out across the pavement, and I had no choice but to stop. Three lanky kids stood at the front. The one in the middle had a black T-shirt on, its Helly Hansen logo was level with my mouth. Their eyes rested on my pockets for a bit, before the one in the black T-shirt looked up and stared right into my face.

OK, what next? Turn and run, or stop and fight? Look like a proper pussy, or get my head kicked in?

I glared up at the kid; come on then mate, let's get on with it.

But just as he took his final step towards me, an older lad appeared behind him and got hold of his shoulder.

'You were hangin' out with Shane the other day, weren't ya?' he said to me.

I nodded.

The younger one glanced at his mate, then back at me. 'Oh, right,' he said after a few seconds. Then him, and all the rest of his mates gradually moved apart, so I could walk straight through.

The next load of kids I saw gave me no bother. The load after that smiled and talked to me a bit. Suddenly, it was like I'd grown about six inch, and I swear down, by the time I'd crossed that estate, met the guy and made the deal, I bounced back to Chapel Cross like a rubber ball.

By the end of that week I'd got myself a growing list of names on my phone and some new G Star jeans. And that's how it more or less carried on over the next few months; deals, laughs, girls and new stuff.

I remember lying in bed one night, wondering what the hell I'd ever been so worried about.

SEVEN

'There's a meeting about you later.'

This was Ruth talking one morning when I went down for something to eat.

'Is there?' I said. 'Why?'

'Well, because you haven't been going to school, have you?'

Bloody hell. I didn't think anybody was really bothering about that. After the exclusion finished, I just sort of never went back, and even though Ruth and Molly made the odd comment every now and again, nobody seemed to be actually doing anything.

'It's at two o'clock this afternoon,' Ruth went on. 'You really ought to be there.'

I took my Coco Pops into the lounge and put the telly on. I'd wagged the odd day from school before loads of times, and maybe a full week every so often, but I'd never missed months at a time like this, and I wasn't really sure what they'd do. I knew some kids who never went at all, but they weren't in care so nobody seemed to bother. But then Shane'd got away with it for long enough, hadn't he? So there must be a way.

'I'd go to the meeting if I were you,' Shane said later when I told him about it. 'Let 'em say their bit, tell ya how clever you are and how well ya could do. Then tell 'em they're right and you'll start goin' again. They'll go away happy, thinkin' how well they've done their jobs. Then you just carry on doin' what ya want; it'll be ages before they get round to sortin' out another meetin'.'

So that's what I did. I sat there at the big table in the dining room at Holly House, with the Head of Year from school, Molly the social worker, some woman from the council and Ruth. I nodded and smiled a lot – but not too much in case they thought I was taking the piss, and I listened to 'em all. I listened to, 'You know you're a really bright lad, Mikey, don't you?' And, 'You've got so much potential, it would be a terrible shame if it went to waste.' And, 'The assessments you've completed so far are all of a really high standard, you could easily attain qualifications in a whole range of subjects ... rhar, rhar, rhar.'

'I suppose you're all right,' I said, when they'd stopped trying to outdo each other in coming up with the wisest, most encouraging thing to say. 'I'll start going again from Monday.'

'That's an excellent decision.' Ruth clapped her hands together. 'I've seen it before when young people stop attending school, it becomes all too easy for them to get in with the wrong crowd and drift into trouble, just because they've got nothing else to do all day.'

'I know what you mean,' I said. 'It's awful when kids end up roaming the streets and dealing drugs and stuff like that. But you've nothing to worry about with me, I promise.'

Before they all left, I managed to get Molly on her own. 'Have you found anythin' out about my brother?' I asked her.

She turned to the last page in the folder she was holding, then skimmed through the notes. 'We've had his records transferred from Leeds, and we've got all the details up until he left local authority care,' she said. 'Then it gets a little more difficult I'm afraid. We have to track down where he went after that. It can take quite a while, Mikey, especially if he's moved around a lot. But we are still working on it and we'll let you know as soon as we find anything out, OK?'

'Yeah, OK.'

Well, that wasn't bad news was it? It wasn't, *yes we've found him and he can't wait to welcome you with open arms into his family and his home*, but on the other hand it wasn't, *he doesn't want to know you and he'll break every bone in your body if you ever try and get in touch with him again*. I could wait.

As she turned away my phone rang. The name that came up was Shane, and I let Molly get out of the door before I answered it.

'Alright?' I said.

'Yeah. Where are ya?'

'The home.'

'Can ya bring us some charlie round to Spots? Donny's over in Manchester and this guy wants a right shedful; he's cleared me and Rocco out.'

I grinned. 'Yeah, OK.'

'Get Corky to bring ya, alright?'

'I'm on my way,' I answered.

After he'd hung up I phoned Corky at the local taxi firm. Him and Donny did a lot of business together and we used him sometimes when we needed to get about a bit quicker than normal. Two minutes later, I got the ring back.

It was still light when I stepped out of the taxi, and I could see Shane, Rocco and this guy standing just round the corner from the snooker club. He was getting on a bit, the guy, and his brown leather jacket was only zipped up at the bottom, cos he was too fat to do it up all the way. I went over and gave the coke to Shane. He checked the amount then looked at the guy, waiting for him to pay.

The guy smiled, felt in his inside pocket, felt in his back pockets, and then in his inside pocket again.

'Bloody 'ell,' he said. 'I must've left my wallet in the car. It's only parked round there.' He pointed to the narrow lane that ran behind the club. 'Do you wanna come with me?'

Shane blinked and looked at Rocco. Rocco glanced up and down the street, then shrugged and nodded. He set off at the side of the guy, and after a couple of seconds me and Shane followed him.

I was staring down as we turned the corner, watching Rocco's Reeboks and the guy's brown leather shoes as they walked along in front of us. The guy was rattling on about some new car he'd bought how much it cost, how fast it could go, shit like that – and Rocco was doing a good job of being impressed. Somehow, these little white flower things had grown up between the cracks in the pavement, and I wondered if the guy was standing on 'em deliberately, or whether it was just a coincidence that he flattened one every time he put his foot down.

It was then though, that he shut up talking. His steps got quicker and I stopped. As I looked up to see him crossing the road, I put my arm out so Shane didn't go any further either. Although Rocco'd slowed right down as well, there was still a fair few yards between him and us. We all watched as the guy got into a light blue Lexus on the opposite side of the road, then our heads shot round.

Four kids, with their hoods up and their faces covered with black scarves, had darted out of an alleyway on Rocco's left. They walked fast but didn't run at first, and as they turned to face us straight on, I saw that every single one of 'em was carrying a long, shining blade.

'Run,' Shane yelled, and he set off like a hare at a dog track.

But I couldn't move; my feet felt like they were stuck in blocks of concrete, and I stood there like an idiot. Rocco whizzed round just as the lads got to him. He took one step towards me, but then his mouth dropped open and he gasped. The kids surrounded him, and for a second I couldn't see what was happening. Then Rocco shoved one of 'em out of the way and he tried hard to take another step. But he had no chance. He stumbled, fell slowly forwards on to the pavement, and then laid there like a kid's Guy Fawkes. Two dark red stains spread quickly across the back of his pale grey hoodie.

The kids paused to look down, then one of 'em, the one nearest to me, lifted his foot up. My whole body stiffened as his orange and black trainer hammered down on to the side of Rocco's head, forcing his shoulders to jerk upwards.

It was then that my legs finally decided to move. Automatically, I started to go towards Rocco. But somebody pulled back hard on my jacket, and when I looked over my shoulder, I saw that Shane'd come back for me.

He spun me around, and dragged me away so fast my feet couldn't keep up. I tripped and almost went down, but Shane just kept on yanking me forward, and somehow I got back up straight.

One of the lads shouted something from behind us then, and my head suddenly cleared. I ran as hard and as fast as I could; just about managing to stay by Shane's side. My arms pumped backwards and forwards and my feet banged down hard on the tarmac, but the sound of the kids' footsteps was close – I mean right close. A sharp pain shot across my chest and my insides felt like they were on fire. Make it to the front of the club, I told myself – just make it to there and they'll leave us alone.

But they didn't. We flew round that corner and hit the main road with no more than six feet between us and them. I stared across at Shane; what now?

Shane hesitated for a split second, then he swerved off to the right and I followed him. Glancing up, I saw what we were running towards and my arms almost fell to my side. I couldn't believe our luck; the taxi, with its hazard lights flashing and engine running, was still parked where it'd dropped me off.

Corky was talking on his mobile, but when me and Shane dove on to the back seat, he realised what was happening and he shot off like a bullet; we must've been a hundred yards down the road before we even shut the doors behind us.

We coughed our guts up and breathed so hard we couldn't speak at first, but as soon as he could, Shane got his phone out and called Donny. He still struggled with his words a bit, but eventually he managed to tell Donny what'd happened. Donny must've asked him a lot of questions, cos Shane kept going over the same stuff, especially about what the old guy looked like.

When they'd finished talking, Shane told Corky to keep going – it didn't matter where, he said, but we'd gotta stay on the move.

I looked at Shane. 'What about Rocco?' I asked him.

'Donny'll make sure he gets an ambulance,' he said, then he turned to me and shrugged. 'There's nowt else we can do.'

'It … it just dun't seem right …' My voice sounded sort of croaky.

'I know …'

I thought Shane was gonna say something else then, something that'd make me feel better. But he didn't. Instead, he turned his head away and stared out of the window.

I looked round and focused on the headlights coming towards us. My eyes were blurry and my head felt sort of heavy. I pictured the guy and the kids who'd jumped us. I pictured the knives, Rocco hitting the ground, that orange and black trainer. If I hadn't have already been sitting down, I think I'd have fainted; honest, it was like a mad cross between a whitey and a bad trip.

When I'd calmed down a bit though, I spoke to Shane again. 'Who do you think they were?'

'Dunno,' Shane said. 'Probably somebody that knows Donny's in Manchester makin' a big deal, and probably somebody that's gonna lose out cos of it. Rocco was unlucky that's all; it could've been any of us – or all of us.'

'D'you think he'll be OK?'

Shane carried on looking out of the window and he didn't answer me for ages, then he shrugged again. 'He were bleedin' proper bad,' he said quietly.

Neither of us talked again until Donny phoned half an hour later and said it was OK for us to go back to the home.

When I laid in bed that night, I knew exactly what I'd been bothered about before. I was bothered Rocco might be dead, I was bothered about how Donny'd take it, and I was bothered cos it could've been me.

Thinking about it all kept me awake most of the night, and I'd only been asleep for a couple of hours when my mobile woke me up again. The ringtone it played was Eminem's *Not Afraid*, and that meant it was Donny.

EIGHT

The other boys were already at the café when me and Shane got there, and we could hear Paulie gobbin' off before we'd even opened the door.

'Pussy bastards,' he said. 'Settin' 'em up like that. I can't believe they got Rocco so easy, and I can't believe him an' the others walked into it like a bunch o' kids …'

Me and Shane looked at each other. Then we knocked, and Paulie shut up as we went in. The sound was down on the telly and it was silent for a few seconds before Donny said, 'You two OK?'

'Yeah,' we nodded together.

'That's good. Tell me what happened again,' he said. 'Right from the beginning.'

Shane told him everything, starting from when he first got the call from the man in the leather jacket.

When he'd finished, Donny said, 'I've asked around a bit – the guy's some relation of Kaler's. From out of town.'

It went quiet again. I looked at my trainers and wondered what Donny was thinking. Him and Kaler went back a long time, and from what I'd heard they'd always had it in for each other. There was loads of history between 'em, but I didn't know if anything like this'd happened before. Was Donny gonna go as mental as I expected?

'So what we gonna do about it?' Paulie's voice made me look up; I could tell he was talking through gritted teeth. 'We can't just let it go. For God's sake, they'll be laughin' at us. I mean, we walked straight into it … and then, we ran straight back out of it.'

He glared at me and Shane as he said that last line, and his eyes made me shudder.

Shane started then, and I was gobsmacked by what he said and how loud he said it.

'Shut your mouth, idiot. What ya sayin' we should've done? Stood there and got cut up like a jigsaw? There were more of 'em and they were waitin' for us. We din't stand a chance, 'specially not once they'd got Rocco. I swear down, if we hadn't run there'd have been three of us layin' there with blood spurtin' out.'

'You had a blade.' Paulie smiled like some villain in a film. 'You too scared to use it? Even to look after a mate?'

Shane flew at him. But Paulie was bigger and he pushed him away like he was a toddler. There was a loud thud as Shane's head hit the wall. He managed to stay on his feet, but Paulie was going after him. I didn't know what to do; Shane still hadn't got his balance back properly and Paulie looked like he was gonna kill him. I took a big breath and stood between 'em.

'There were nothin' we coulda done,' I said, as loud as I could manage.

'Shift,' Paulie yelled in my face.

But I didn't move. I stared up at him and watched as his eyes got narrower. My fingers curled up to make two fists and I opened my mouth to say something else – then didn't. Jesus, what now? Obviously he could've murdered me if he'd wanted to, but I don't think either of us really knew what to do next.

Then Donny stood up. 'Leave it,' he said.

Paulie glared at me, then at Shane, then he turned away. I started to breathe again, and as I stretched my fingers back out, I could see the red marks where my nails had dug into the palm of my hands.

Paulie shook his head and slammed himself down into a chair. 'Well if them two couldn't do nowt, we'd better make sure somebody else does. They'll think they've got away with it.'

'They're not gonna get away with nothin'.' Donny's voice was steady and even quieter than normal. 'But we're gonna wait. We're gonna wait 'til Rocco gets out, then we'll sort it.'

Shane came to stand next to me and we glanced at each other.

Donny walked over to the window. 'We gotta watch our backs,' he said. 'Stick together as much as you can, stay away from Spots where all the cops are, and you two take these.'

My eyes must've doubled in size as I watched him get two guns out of a drawer and give one to Paulie and the other to Shane. Shane didn't even look at it before he put it in his inside pocket, and it was obvious he'd had one before.

'Don't use 'em unless you need to,' Donny said. 'Not yet.'

His face set like rock then. I could see his chest going up and down with every breath he took, and when he sat back down and turned the volume up on the telly, we all walked out.

***

Me and Shane stayed together all day just like Donny said. We kept well inside our area, and if we could, we got people to come to us. Usually we'd meet 'em pretty much wherever they wanted, but for now we had to keep things extra safe.

As we walked back towards Holly House that afternoon, we talked about Rocco properly for the first time.

'How we gonna find out if he's OK?' I asked Shane.

'Well we're not gonna buy him flowers an' grapes and go an' sit round his hospital bed, that's for sure.'

He smiled, then stopped messing about. 'Don't worry. Donny'll get to know, he always gets to know stuff.'

'What d'you think he'll do about it?'

Shane shrugged. 'Depends, dunnit? If Rocco dun't make it or if there's any more agro from Kaler, then he'll go after 'em big time. But if Rocco's OK and things stay quiet for a bit, Donny'll be more easy on 'em. That dun't mean he won't do owt at all though; he proper hates them Kalers, and he'll use owt as an excuse to have a go. He even hates like their little kids, or anybody that hangs out with 'em; I saw him glass this bird once just cos she'd shacked up with one of their boys.'

I frowned. I knew Donny could be a bit of a psycho sometimes, but that?

Shane looked at me, nodded his head slightly, then

shrugged again. 'Suppose we'll just have to wait an' see what happens next,' he said.

It was all I could think about as we walked on. I really hoped Rocco was gonna be OK. He was a sound kid who'd do anything for his mates, and I wanted him to get better; I wanted him to be around again. But apart from that, I was proper on edge about what'd kick off if he didn't pull through. Donny was right mad about what'd happened. I know it wasn't him who got knifed, but it was him who they were really having a go at. If Rocco died, Kaler's lot were gonna have to pay – and it'd be us who were collecting the debt.

Me and Shane turned a corner then and we stopped dead. In the distance, just outside the home, there was a brand new silver Audi; the windows were blacked out and its engine was running. We backed up against the wall and looked at each other, then we checked all round us, but everything else was normal.

'D'you think it's them?' I whispered.

Shane didn't take his eyes off the car. 'Dunno. I don't recognise it,' he said slowly, and he brought his hand up and slid it into his inside pocket.

We stared at the car for what seemed like ages. Its lights stayed on and a thin line of smoke came out of the exhaust.

'I'll phone Donny and see if he knows owt,' Shane said eventually, and he got his phone out with his other hand.

But just as he was about to make the call, the driver's door began to open. I tapped Shane on his sleeve and nodded at the car.

'We'd betta chip,' Shane said, and he turned away.

I started to follow him, but then I took one last glance back – and that's when I saw her. A grey-haired woman wearing a pink flowery skirt had got out of the car, and she was standing there straightening her matching jacket. She was one of the social workers who came to Holly House sometimes, but she'd never turned up in that car before. I began to laugh, then Shane began to laugh, and it went on for so long I'm surprised neither of us peed ourselves.

When we'd finally shut up, we carried on walking towards the home, but then Shane stopped again. For God's sake, I thought, what now? I followed his eyes and I soon knew what. A lass'd just got out of the passenger side of the Audi. She was standing on the pavement holding a bag and staring up at the house, and she was so hot you could've made toast on her.

I looked back at Shane. He wasn't blinking and he had this soppy expression on his face that I'd never seen before. I rolled my eyes up to the sky and shook my head. And then I grinned. 'Is that a gun in your pocket,' I whispered. 'Or are you just pleased to see her?'

NINE

The new girl was standing just inside the house when we got in, and she really was a darling. She was little – petite – that's the word. Her eyes were the same colour as Galaxy chocolate, and she had this dark wavy hair that went right down to her backside.

Ruth was doing the usual, 'This's the kitchen, rhar, rhar, rhar ….' But she stopped when she saw us, and said to the lass, 'Jasmine, this is Shane and this is Mikey. They live here too.'

I smiled, and Shane said hello as though he was talking to some kind of princess – but Jasmine still looked at us like we were a pack of snarling dogs, and she was a baby deer.

'Come on, let me show you around upstairs,' Ruth said to her.

Jasmine bowed her head so her hair fell over her face, then gripping her bag with both hands, she inched round us and followed Ruth into the hall.

Shane stared after her like a puppy that'd had its bone taxed.

I smirked. 'God, what if that's it, mate? What if you never see her again?'

'No, no, it's alright; she's only gone upstairs,' he said seriously. 'I'll just have to hang about a bit 'til she comes back down.'

I shook my head, and he didn't even notice when I strolled off into the lounge and started looking round for the remote control.

She was gorgeous, there was no doubt about it. I

mean like, tongue out, mouth drooling, knee wobblingly gorgeous. If Shane hadn't fallen for her like Posh'd fallen for Becks, it would've been me standing in that kitchen right now.

But I'd never seen him act like that before, ever. And, although I got my fair share of the action, I knew I didn't stand much of a chance against Shane anyway; it was like asking her to choose between Haagen Dazs double choc-chip and school dinner sprouts.

So I decided to leave him to it. To be honest, I didn't reckon either of us would ever get very far with her. As well as being gorgeous, she was also terrified; terrified of being here, and terrified of us. Even Shane the Super Stud was gonna have to work proper hard on this one, and it was probably gonna be more of a laugh just sitting back and watching him.

The remote was in a plant pot, and after I'd knocked the soil off it, I stretched out on the settee and got comfy. The telly'd just flicked on when Shane's phone sounded from the kitchen, then the lounge door burst open so fast I'd jumped halfway back up again before I saw his face in the doorway.

'He's OK!' Shane said, waving his phone about in the air. 'Rocco's OK – I mean not OK, but like, ya know … he's not gonna die.'

'Well thank God for that!' I laughed, and let myself fall back against the cushion. 'How d'you know?'

'Paulie sent their lass round to Rocco's mum's – got her to phone up and find out what were happenin'. He's still like proper poorly, but they said he weren't critical anymore – so that's good, yeah?'

'Yeah, that's good.'

'Cool. Can't wait to see him, wonder – '

Shane went quiet as the floorboards at the bottom of the stairs told us somebody was treading on 'em. He peered round into the hall, then scowled when he realised Ruth was on her own. Without looking at me again, he mumbled, 'Just … gonna ... see …' and wandered out.

Oh yes, I smiled; this was gonna be fun.

I went back to looking at the telly, but thought about Rocco. Good old lad; I knew it'd take more than a few of those Kalers to finish him off.

**

Well, if Shane had waited in the kitchen 'til Jasmine came back down, he'd still've been there a week later. I'm not sure how she managed it, but I swear down, Jasmine stayed in that bedroom twenty four seven when she first got to the home.

The reason I know she never came out, is because a) Shane kept telling me every two minutes, and b) we were stuck in that bloody house nearly all the time. Although the cops'd concentrated on the area round Bank Street when Rocco'd first got knifed, they soon spread out, and suddenly there were more high vis coats in S16 than there were at a Wednesday/United derby. You couldn't even poke your cap out of the front door without getting searched – which, obviously, was a right pain in the arse for me and Shane. We had no choice but to keep our heads down, stay inside Holly

House, and deal with all that frickin free time.

I used a lot of mine up phoning Molly and listening to her voicemail recordings. If she wasn't out of the office, then she was in a meeting or on annual leave. I did start off leaving messages, but soon realised it was pointless – like I said to Shane, I was more likely to get a call from Cheryl Cole than I was from her.

Leon was in my head constantly. I tried hard not to obsess about what it'd be like to find him, and see him, and hear him talk, cos I knew it might all never happen. But I thought about it anyway; it was like those images just snuck into my mind whenever I wasn't on guard.

Shane, of course, had other thoughts in his head. He'd been living for the click of Jasmine's door opening for over a week, so by the time it finally did, he was pretty much on his last legs.

Funny thing is, we almost missed it. It was one afternoon when it seemed like things were starting to get back to normal, and me and Shane decided to risk an outing. We walked around then hung about a bit, but even though there weren't as many cops around, people were still proper cagey. The streets were dead and our phones hardly rang. After about an hour, we decided to go back.

We opened the backdoor into the kitchen just as Jasmine walked into it from the hall. She froze, and made a noise like she'd just seen a six foot tarantula. And as Shane stopped, and checked out her black vest-top with a picture of Mini Mouse on it, and her tight, pale, cropped jeans, his eyes grew as big as Frisbees.

She stared at us for a couple of seconds, then went to

go back upstairs.

'Are you alright?' Shane asked quickly.

Jasmine stopped and turned back steadily. She glanced at him, then lowered her eyes before she answered. 'I was just going to get something to eat, but it's OK; I'm not really hungry.' Her voice was all shy and right soft.

Shane pulled his hood down. 'I'll take you out for somethin' if ya like? Pizza, curry, whatever ya want?'

She had two silver bangles round her wrist, and they clinked together as she pushed her hair back off her face and let her eyes float upwards. 'I ... err ...' She hesitated, looked out of the window, then back at the floor. 'It's alright – like I said, I'm not really hungry.'

There was a pause where nobody knew what to say, then Jasmine raised her head and gazed straight at Shane. 'Thanks, though,' she said, and she smiled the most lovely, kind, sparkly smile you've ever seen in your life.

Jesus, she made *me* gulp a bit as she walked away. Her bare arms swung slightly at her side, and her long hair swayed in time with her hips. When I looked back at Shane though, I nearly cracked up. If he'd have been in a cartoon, his eyes would've turned into big red love hearts, his tongue would've rolled out of his mouth and stretched down to his knees, and his heart would've bust out of his chest then bounced backwards and forwards on the end of a spring.

'Did ya see that?' he said.

'Yeah, mate; I saw it.'

He sighed. 'I swear down, I am so gonna – '

'Ah, Mikey, you're back,' Ruth came out of the office and stood in the doorway. 'Molly's just phoned, she wants you to give her a ring.'

I gawped at her. 'What does she want? Is it about Leon?'

'She didn't say. She's only going to be in the office for another half an hour though, so ...'

I didn't hear the rest; I pushed past her and snatched up the phone in the office. I knew Molly's number like I knew my name, and as the phone rang and rang and rang, I'm not sure what raced fastest; my mind or my heart. Finally, there was a click, a silence, then she answered.

'It's Mikey,' I said.

'Hello. Yes, you left me a message, asking me to contact you?'

I flopped down in a chair behind me – that didn't sound like she had anything exciting to tell me, did it?

'I left you bare messages,' I said. 'I want to know if there's anything new about Leon.'

'Oh, right. Let me just have a quick look.' I heard her tip-tapping on a keyboard, and although she didn't actually come back with, 'Computer says no,' she might as well've done.

'Erm, it looks like we've managed to find the address of the first place he lived on his own, but that was a long time ago, and apparently he didn't stay there long. So now we're trying to establish where he went afterwards.'

I sank down further. 'Is that it? Nothin' else?'

'Not at the moment, I'm afraid. I'll keep you

informed though.'

Yeah, course you will, I thought, but I managed not to say it.

I let the phone fall to the floor, got up, and went straight out of the front door.

They weren't gonna find him, were they? He was one guy in this huge bleeding world; what were the odds? Slim? Miniscule? Nonexistent?

He could be anywhere, abroad even. He could've changed his name, he could be ... dead. And, although he was big and important to me, to them, he was nothing. I mean, how hard were they even trying?

I jumped down the bottom three steps and pushed the wheely-bin over.

So, what would I do if they never found out where he was? It was worse than before. Being on my own was shit, but being on my own and knowing my brother was out there somewhere, knowing I couldn't see him and that he had no idea I was even alive; I'm not sure I could live with that.

When I got to the end of the road, I turned in the direction of the off-license, and it was just as I was draining my second can of Magners, that Shane phoned.

'Where are ya, mate?' he asked.

'Outside Frankie's.'

'You OK? Was it bad news?'

'Nah ... it were no news at all really.'

'Well, they say that's good, don't they? And, at least she called ya back. Cheryl'll probably be next – I'd best get off the phone quick.'

I smiled, then Shane said, 'Wait there. I'll come

round to ya, yeah?'

'OK,' I said, and a few minutes later he was standing next to me with cider running down the outside of the can and all over his fingers.

'So, did you get any further with Jasmine?' I said after a while.

He slurped the Magners off the back of his hand and shook his head. 'I were thinking of goin' up to her room and tryin' to talk to her, but I din't.'

'Why?'

Shane looked at me. 'Ahh, maybe the time weren't right,' he said.

I took a long swig and wondered what he was on about. Then, I realised – what he meant was, he'd come to find me instead.

I nearly said something; cheers, or something like that. But Shane smiled. 'Come on,' he said. 'I haven't kicked your ass at pool for ages.' And after he'd volleyed the empty can into somebody's garden, we set off for The Forge, the most minging pub in S16.

TEN

I didn't get out of bed for two full days after that – can you believe it? Two, whole, long, days? I tried to make out I was proper ill, but everybody ignored me and said it was a hangover, and I got absolutely no sympathy whatsoever. In fact, I think they played the music that loud and hoovered my bedroom so often, just to piss me off.

When I did get up, it was because the smoke detectors on the landing went crazy. I buried my head in my pillow and held the duvet over my ears for as long as I could, but eventually that high pitched screech became way too much.

I knew it'd be one of the freaky twins. They'd either have had a fag in their bedroom, or left their straighteners on, or set fire to their carpet – which'd all happened before. Me and Shane used to just take the batteries out, but then we got proper done off the guy with the ginger beard, and he screwed them all shut after that.

As I'd hoped, it was a bit quieter downstairs, and when I went into the kitchen, Shane was making his dinner.

'Hey,' he said. 'You're conscious an' everythin'.'

'Yeah, everythin',' I said, staring at his beef-spread and saladcream sandwich, and realising I needed to get back to bed smartish.

'You were in a right tangle,' he laughed, and he threw a beef-spread-covered knife into the sink. The clatter made me wince.

'I'm surprised you've even made it up now.' He bit into the sandwich, and saladcream oozed out of the sides.

I closed my eyes and turned my head away before I opened 'em again. 'It's only cos of the smoke alarms. I thought they were gonna bust my head open; I couldn't stand it in that room anymore.'

Shane wiped his chin with his hand as I looked back round. 'Mmm, wish they'd have the same affect on Jasmine,' he said.

'Still no show?'

'Nope. I even wondered if they'd moved her out, but then I saw that black top in the dryer this mornin'. It's not right though is it – stayin' in like that? I wonder what's up with her?'

'Why don't you go and ask her?' I said, breathing slowly to try and keep my stomach still.

'Oh yeah, right. I'll just go walkin' in there and say, *''scuse me love, but I can't help noticin' you've got a bit of a social problem, in that you don't socialise. Now come on, snap out of it, cos otherwise you're gonna get yourself a name for being a right mardy cow.'* She'd probably bang me out!'

I laughed. 'Well you don't say that, do you. You go in and be all kind and caring and ask her if she'd like somebody to talk to, somebody to show her around, rhar, rhar, rhar. You can do that …' I paused for a second. 'You were the only one who was alright with me when I first got here.'

'Yeah, but it were easy bein' alright with you; you're not female or fit.'

'No, but all your other gals are.'

'They're not like her,' Shane said, and he looked at what was left of the sandwich, then lobbed it in the bin.

'Oh, for God's sake, just go an' talk to her – if you don't, I will, and then you'll look like a right loser.'

Shane laughed a bit, then took a deep breath. 'You think I should?'

I nodded just as the noise from the alarms stopped. 'See, it's even gone quiet for you.'

He wiped his hands down his jeans, then went and started to climb the stairs.

'Knock first,' I shouted after him, and when I heard his footsteps on the landing, I couldn't help sneaking halfway up the stairs to hear what happened.

He remembered to knock, and after a few seconds she opened the door.

'Err, I just wondered if you were OK,' he said, more softly than I'd ever heard him talk before.

'Oh … yeah, I'm OK,' Jasmine replied. 'It's nice of you to come and ask.'

He must've gone into her room then, cos the door closed and it all went quiet.

I smiled. Well thank God for that; at least now he might stop looking so bloody miserable all the time.

I realised that my head'd stopped hurting then, so instead of going back to bed, I decided to get out for a bit. I'd just got to the bottom of the stairs though, when Ruth collared me. She'd been talking to one of the freaky twins in the lounge, but the door was open, and as soon as she saw me in the hall, she started.

'They've been on the phone again, Mikey, about you

not going to school.'

'Me? I hope you told 'em I haven't been very well.'

She tutted. 'They're not just talking about the last few days; they're concerned about the last few months.'

'It hasn't been that long.'

'Oh yes it has. You said at that meeting you were going to start attending again, and you haven't been once since'

'OK, OK, I'll start going again, promise.'

'I hope so, Mikey, because otherwise we'll have to start withholding some of your weekly allowance.'

Oooh, withholding my weekly allowance!

I could make my weekly allowance standing on my head with my hands tied behind my back in about twenty minutes working for Donny. She didn't have a clue.

I smiled a big smile and nodded. 'I'll go, honest. I'll be there tomorrow.'

Then I opened the front door and left her to it.

'I really hope you mean it,' she shouted.

But we both knew there was more chance of me sitting in Chapel Cross library than sitting in school the next day, and Chapel Cross library had been shut for two years.

***

When I saw Shane in Previews later that night, he looked like somebody off a toothpaste advert.

'Aah, look at you, all loved up,' I yelled over the

music.

'Shut it, you idiot,' he shouted back, still grinning.

'Surprised you've managed to drag yourself away, or did she give you the big E?'

'Course not mate. She's well keen – she wouldn't be waitin' up for me otherwise, would she?' Shane winked and the grin nearly reached his ears.

We were busy that night. Everybody was finally surfacing again, and they were more than making up for lost time. The tunes were cool and loud, and except for a couple of lasses who started throwing broken glasses about, everything else was pretty chilled. After a few hours, my pile of notes was so thick I had to spread it out – there was cash in every pocket I'd got. Wish it was all mine, I thought, as I caught up with Shane and we made our way out.

It was proper late by then. My eyes were stinging, and all I could think about as we walked home was flopping into bed and knocking out the zeds. Shane was still buzzin' though, and as we went along he rattled on and messed about balancing on walls and kicking cans around.

Then his phone rang.

'Yeah?' he said. 'Yeah, he's here … OK.'

Shane's smile disappeared for the first time in three hours.

'Donny?' I asked him.

He nodded.

'Does he want us now?'

'Yep,' Shane said, and he looked up at the sky and breathed out hard. 'He's over at The Forge.'

So we turned on our heels and went in the opposite direction, and this time as we walked along, Shane was as quiet as a corpse.

Cos it was way past closing time, we went into the pub through the backdoor. Tommy, who ran it, was cashing-up in what the regulars called the 'best side' – in what way 'best', it's hard to tell. True, you could see glimpses of carpet between all the fag-burns and chuddy, and, some of the tables even had specks of varnish left on, but it was still pretty minging.

Tommy was the only person in there, so we went through into the other side, where we could hear the thud of pool balls being potted. Paulie and Jake had the cues in their hands, and Donny, who was smiling like Ronald McDonald, stood watching 'em. Standing next to him, was Rocco.

'Hey,' said Shane, as he went and put his hand on Rocco's shoulder. 'How ya doin'?'

'I'm good, yeah,' said Rocco, smiling.

He didn't seem too great though. He was swaying about and he looked like he could pass out any second. His face was pale and you could see the sweat on his top lip.

'Good to see you,' I said. 'You sure you should be out though?'

'They didn't want me to, but I'd had enough, mate. Grub were crap. D'ya wanna see what they did?'

Before any of us could answer, Rocco pulled his T-shirt up, turned to the side and showed us the knife wounds. There were two cuts that were about three or four centimetres long, they were bright red and all stitched up.

Rocco pointed to the cut that was highest. 'That's the one that punctured my lung,' he said. 'The other's not that deep, but there's one on the top of my leg that goes right down to the bone.'

Bloody hell – now it was my turn to sway and get a sweaty face. He really had been cut up proper bad.

'You oughta sit down,' Donny said, and it took me a second to realise he meant Rocco and not me.

Rocco eased himself into one of the alcoves and Donny went to get him a drink. While Donny'd got his back to us, me and Shane looked at each other, wondering why this couldn't have waited 'til tomorrow.

Donny handed Rocco the whiskey or brandy or whatever it was, then nobody spoke for a bit. When I glanced over at Rocco again though, his eyes were shut tight and he was gripping the glass right hard.

'You alright?' I said, and I went and knelt down next to his chair.

Rocco forced himself to smile for a second. 'I guess it must be time for some more painkillers, mate,' he said, and I could hear his teeth grating together.

'Take him home will you?' Donny got his car keys out of his pocket and threw them over to Jake.

'Sure,' Jake said as he caught the keys, and me and him gave Rocco a hand up.

I watched 'em walk out and I shuddered; Rocco could hardly lift his feet off the floor. It made me think about the cuts he'd showed us. They were serious enough as it was, but what if they'd been deeper? Or a bit to the left, or a bit higher? What if they'd gone into his heart, or if he'd bled more, or if the ambulance had taken longer to get there? He'd have been dead, that's what.

After they'd gone out, I hoped we'd be able to chip as well, but Donny seemed to want us to stay.

'What do you think?' he said, without looking at any of us.

Shane answered first, thank God.

'Whatever we do, we're gonna have to be proper careful – cos they're gonna be expectin' summat. We've gotta plan it real well.'

Donny nodded once then looked at Paulie.

'Shoot 'em,' Paulie said with a shrug.

I started to laugh. Not cos it was funny – obviously the last thing on Paulie's mind was cracking jokes – but you know when you get that right nervous feeling in your stomach, and it makes you laugh cos you don't know what else to do? Well that's how I felt, and that's why I had to put my hand over my mouth and try and make the laugh sound like a cough.

Paulie glared at me. His eyes were always sort of little and hard, but as he looked at me then, they burned like two fag ends. I managed to shut up and I focused on an empty Carling can that was crushed up on the floor.

Shane glanced at Paulie, then me, then he spoke to Donny quickly. 'So what are we gonna do?' he said.

Donny sat down and tapped his fingers on the table in front of him. 'We're gonna have a little trip over to S22 one night soon,' he said. 'One night when we know there'll be a few of 'em together. At first, we'll take it steady; get 'em exactly where we want 'em.' Donny paused before he went on in a voice we could hardly hear. 'And then, we'll make 'em look like Rocco looks.'

After a second, he jumped back up. 'Think about it and be at the café tomorrow afternoon.'

He phoned Corky then, and ten minutes later me and Shane walked into Holly House.

Sometimes we went in separately so they didn't know whether we'd been together or not, but that night we just couldn't be arsed, and the staff who were on gave us a right roasting. We were both too knackered to argue though, and we made our way upstairs as quickly as we could.

I opened my bedroom door, got halfway in, then stopped to see where Shane went. He was standing on the landing, leaning over the stairs to check if the staff were around. When he was sure they weren't, he knocked quietly on Jasmine's door. It opened straightaway and he went in.

OK for some, I thought.

I went and laid on the bed then and stared up at the cracks in the cream coloured ceiling.

So, we're going over to their area, in a few days' time probably.

I wondered what I'd have to do. I was still fairly new to it all, wasn't I? Maybe I'd be on the edges, you know, lookout or something like that? But then again who knows? Donny'd want to hit as many of 'em as he could; so he'd use as many of us as he could.

Don't get me wrong, I knew we had to get 'em back. We had to show 'em they couldn't mess with us.

But I just didn't know how it'd all turn out.

ELEVEN

'Mikey, wake up. Come on, open your eyes.'

I heard the voice, I recognised it as Ruth's, but the last thing I could do was wake up. There was just no way my eyes were gonna open; they felt like they were nailed shut.

I turned over, pulled the warm duvet up round my shoulders and snuggled my head deep into the pillow.

'Mikey! I need to talk to you.'

'What the … Not now,' I said, starting to drift off again.

'Well you won't be saying that when you know what I know.'

I sighed. I know it'll be a load of crap, I thought. But my mind wouldn't settle back down after that. 'Go on then, what's up?'

'Oh, you need to be properly awake to listen to this.' Ruth's voice was high and cheerful, and as she spoke she went over to open the curtains.

The bright light made me screw my eyes up even tighter, but then I blinked a few times, and forced one and then the other eyelid gradually open.

Slowly, Ruth came into focus.

'I've just spoken to Molly,' she said, smiling. 'Guess what?'

'What?' I said without thinking.

But then my brain fired up. And I did think, and I sat up in bed and yelled, 'Leon? Have they found him?'

Ruth laughed and nodded.

My hands quivered like mad; I didn't know what to

do with 'em, but I just couldn't keep 'em still. 'Have they talked to him? Does he want to see me? Where is he?'

'Yes they've spoken to him, and yes he's looking forward to meeting you …'

'Really? Wick-ed!' I jumped out of bed and did this stupid dance thing all round the room.

'Whoa … will you get some clothes on?' Ruth said, turning her head away and putting her hand up to cover her eyes.

I looked down. My boxers were perfectly in place – what was wrong with her?

'So where is he then?' I asked.

'Clothes!' she said, still not looking round.

I grabbed my jeans and a T-shirt and pulled them on. 'OK, you're safe.'

Ruth turned to me, but her smile was different now, it was sort of fake. 'They have located him, but, well, he's in Dalton prison.'

'Oh,' I said, taking it in steadily. 'How long for?'

'I don't know; I'm not sure of all the details yet. But Molly is sorting out a visit for you as soon as possible, and like I said, apparently he was really pleased about the news. He can't wait to see you.'

I sat back down on the bed. So, my brother wants to meet me. He's pleased I exist. I'm actually gonna see him, and soon. I squeezed my hands together hard.

But then I wondered how come he'd got banged up in the first place? Had he done something proper bad?

I shook the thought out of my head. Nah, it won't be much. I bet he'll be out in a few months. Then I'll be able to see him all the time. It'll all be fine.

'When will the visit be?' I asked Ruth.

'Hopefully within the next week,' she said. 'Molly's phoning back this afternoon, as soon as she's had her lunch.' She looked down at her watch, 'In fact, any time now.'

'It's the afternoon already?' I said, looking up. And for the first time since I'd opened my eyes, I thought about Donny and Rocco, and I remembered I needed to be somewhere else.

***

They were all at the café except for Donny when I got there. Paulie and Jake were watching the telly, and Shane was looking at his phone. 'I was just gonna call you,' he said quietly, as he put it away.

'I've been – '

The backdoor opened and Donny walked in with a lad close behind him. I'd seen him a couple of times before, the kid, but I didn't really know him that well. He was called Tyler, and he nodded at Jake and went and stood next to him.

Donny scanned the room, then got himself comfortable in his big leather chair. He looked in Paulie's direction, and said, 'Benjy Kaler's house, Thursday nights ... three or four of 'em play poker.'

Paulie's eyes grew more suspicious than normal. 'Who told ya?'

'Somebody that knows,' Donny said, and the edge in his voice made me glad he wasn't talking to me. Paulie lit a cigarette and looked down before Donny carried on. 'If we can get 'em all out on the road, it'll be easy.'

Easy? What, exactly, was gonna be easy? What was he thinking?

'We could get somebody to call 'em,' Tyler said. 'Tell 'em one of their boys is in trouble?'

Donny thought about it, then shook his head. 'They'd be suspicious if somebody they didn't know called 'em. And, even if they did go for it, they'd come out all tooled up.'

'What about their cars?' Jake said. 'Them Kalers love their cars. If we smash one of 'em in, they'll be out of that house quicker than a rat out of fire, and, they might not stop to pick owt up.'

Tyler got all excited. 'Yeah, you're right. We'd have to make sure they knew we were doin' it though; you know, get 'em lookin' out of their window or summat like that?'

It was quiet for a while. I could see how smashing their car in would get 'em out of the house, but it'd also mean they were blazing mad about it. Was that a good time to be doing whatever we were gonna do?

The sound of a woman laughing right loud came from the café. Shane turned his head. 'Somebody could go to their door,' he said.

Paulie glanced up for the first time since Donny'd talked to him. 'Bit old for knock-a-door-run aren't ya?'

'I'm not sayin' it has to be one of us.' Shane ignored Paulie and spoke directly to Donny. 'It could be anybody; somebody deliverin' somethin' maybe?'

Donny nodded, then his eyes flitted across and

landed on me. Jeez, what was I gonna add to it all? I dug around like crazy trying to come up with something to add, but there was nothing; I couldn't think of a single idea that didn't sound stupid.

Donny soon realised it, thank God, and he reached his hand up, rubbed his forehead and closed his eyes.

Shane looked my way. 'It's OK,' he mouthed silently.

Paulie's phone rang then. Before the caller'd even had chance to say a word though, Paulie said, 'I'll call ya back in a bit,' and hung up.

Donny opened his eyes again. 'Right. Next Thursday. You'll be able to TWOC a couple of cars, yeah?' He nodded at Tyler.

'Yeah, sure,' Tyler said.

'Sound. We'll drive across in them. A kid I know delivers for Akbar's; I'll get him to take a curry over to Kaler's at eleven. While they're on the doorstep tellin' him they haven't ordered it, we'll drive one of our cars into one of theirs. They'll see it, come runnin' out ... and that's when we'll hit 'em.'

His fingers still touched his forehead, and he moved 'em round slightly 'til the side of his head rested on his hand. 'What d'you think?'

I joined in with all the nodding and noises that showed we thought it was a solid idea. Only Paulie stayed quiet and still.

'You not sure?' Donny asked him, and it was like he really cared what the answer was.

Paulie rolled his fag end against the wall until it went out. He stared at it, then crumbled it up in his

104

fingers. 'I think it'll probably work,' he said, and a thin smile spread across his face.

Shane looked up at the clock then. 'I err, gotta meet somebody. Is that OK?'

'Yeah, I gotta get goin' myself,' Donny said, and he left through the back, as I tried to keep up with Shane as he raced through the café.

He turned and talked to me before I had chance to ask him any of the questions that were queuing up in my head. 'I'm meetin' Jasmine from school,' he whispered. 'Can ya take care of things for a bit?'

'Yeah, course.'

I watched him walk away and supposed my questions'd just have to wait.

***

A few calls did come through, but then it went quiet, so I decided to go back to the house to chill for a couple of hours.

I got something to eat and went into the lounge to watch MTV, but the telly'd gone – again. Oh I know that'll probably seem a bit strange to you, but every so often, the telly at Holly House vanished. It was the freaky twins. Whenever they thought they could get away with it, they just picked the telly up and walked out with it. Then they'd flog it for a few quid and spend the money on weed – which me or Shane supplied with a smile.

So I sat there and stared at the TV stand while I ate my tea. Although I'd got two pretty big things to think about, I couldn't really concentrate on either of 'em. The thought of meeting Leon made my insides jump with excitement one minute and screw-up with nerves the next, and if I'm honest, I was proper shitting myself about the thing with the Kalers.

Donny'd said 'we', when he'd talked to us, hadn't he? But I was fairly sure he really meant 'you'. I'd eat my cap if he was there with us. And I still wasn't really sure what he wanted us to do. I mean, I know we weren't gonna be tapping 'em on the shoulders and saying, *''Scuse me old bean, but it's really not on, stabbing one of our chaps when we were outnumbered. We'd appreciate it if you wouldn't do it again.'* I mean, I know it was gonna be serious. But how far, exactly, was he gonna go ...?

I started to play Tetris on my phone to take my mind off everything, but it didn't really work, and I was just about to get up and do something, do anything, when Shane and Jasmine walked in.

'Alright, mate?' Shane said, and he glanced round the room. 'Telly's gone walkabouts again then?'

'Yeah,' I smiled. Then just for something to say, I added, 'Where you been?'

'Film an' a pizza,' he answered, as he flopped down on the settee next to Jasmine.

I wasn't looking at 'em properly, but out of the corner of my eye I saw him take hold of her hand and he sat there stroking it the whole time.

I carried on playing the game. It was quiet without the TV on, and it felt a bit awkward at first, but then Shane said, 'Did Ruth find ya this morning? She were in a right flap in case you'd already gone out.'

'Yeah, I talked to her.'

'And …? Go on then, what did she want?'

I hadn't planned to spill my guts out about Leon to anybody, especially not to Jasmine who I'd only known for two minutes. But once I started, I just couldn't stop, and I ended up telling 'em everything.

'That's wicked,' Shane said when I finally shut up. 'I bet he'll be a proper sound guy.'

'Yeah,' I said, and I tried hard to control the grin that was spreading across my face.

'You must be really pleased?' This was from Jasmine and we both looked at her – it was the first time she'd said a word since they'd come in.

She smiled, and you didn't have to be a genius to work out why Shane couldn't take his eyes off her – she was like more stunning than ever.

'I hope he turns out to be better than my brothers; they're all complete idiots,' she went on softly, and her eyes dropped down.

Shane let go of her hand and put his arm round her shoulder instead. He pulled her closer to him, leaned over and kissed the top of her head.

Ruth came in then, and Jasmine jumped up like a startled kitten.

'I'll see you later,' Jasmine said quickly, and she smiled again and went.

Shane watched her right 'til she disappeared out of the door.

'Oh, it's good to see she's settling in and feeling happier.' Ruth paused, then looked at me. 'That meeting we talked about this morning, Mikey? It's arranged for Friday. Molly's going to pick you up at nine, OK?

'Thanks,' I said.

'When do we get a new telly?' Shane asked her.

'When somebody has the time to go and buy one, I suppose.'

'It's crap without it,' Shane said. 'There's nowt to do.'

'You hardly watch it when it's here.' Ruth's voice got more stroppy. 'And anyway, if you're not happy about it, go and speak to the people who took it.'

Shane beamed at her. 'Tell ya what, give us forty quid an' I'll go an' buy it back for ya.'

'Mmm,' Ruth raised her eyebrows. 'Give *you* forty pounds? Do you think I was born yesterday?'

'Well not yesterday maybe, but with your youthful looks an' cheerful personality, it can't be that long ago.' He winked at her. 'Go on, forty quid; you know it makes sense.'

Ruth's face broke into a smile and she walked out of the lounge shaking her head.

When the door'd closed behind her, I thought again about what she'd said. 'Friday,' I said quietly, as much to myself as to Shane.

'Yeah. Not long,' he said.

'If things don't go right Thursday night though …?

'It'll be OK.'

'It's just …' I didn't finish what I wanted to say – it would've sounded stupid.

'It will be OK,' Shane said again, and he got up.

'Come on, let's go into town and –'

He stopped talking and sighed as The Simpsons' theme tune played on his phone. It was one of the regulars, and when he'd sorted out where to meet him, Shane looked at me again.

'Tomorrow,' he said, as he pulled his hood up. 'We'll go out an' treat ourselves.'

I nodded and managed to smile as he passed me on his way out.

Left on my own, it wasn't long before it all started going round in my head again. Friday was the day I'd been waiting for all my life; it was the day I'd been waiting for since before I even knew Leon existed.

But I had to get through Thursday night first, didn't I? And if anything went wrong – if I ended up in custody, or in hospital, or … dead – then that'd be it.

And I mean it could happen, couldn't it? Any one of those things could happen easily.

Was there a way out of it, I wondered? Was there anything I could do to get round it? Maybe I could pretend to be poorly? But then what illness would be so bad I couldn't show up on Thursday night, and yet be cured by Friday morning so I could still make the visit? Donny'd never buy it.

And really, deep down, I knew I'd never bottle it anyway – for two reasons: one, I wouldn't let Shane and Rocco down. We had to get even for what they'd done to Rocco, and there was no way I'd sit back and watch Shane go without me. And two, Donny'd go psycho. He'd think I'd gone soft and turned into some kind of pussy. He'd be disappointed, and it could end up being more dangerous to stay away, than it would be to turn up.

I closed my eyes. Let's just get it over and done with, I thought.

***

The next day I walked round to Donny's and we went through all the usual stuff. When we'd done though, I took my time sorting the packs out and putting 'em into my pockets.

He sat down and started to cut some charlie, but when I still didn't go, he stopped and looked at me.

'What's up, Mikey?' he asked.

'I, err, I just wanted to tell you – to ask you I mean – if it's OK if I'm not around much on Friday?'

'That's no problem.' He smiled. 'What you got planned?'

I told him about Leon. I missed out some of the details, but I told him what he needed to know.

'That's really cool,' he said when I'd finished. 'It must mean a lot to you to have found him?'

I nodded.

'Where's he in?' Donny said.

'Dalton.'

'What wing?'

'I'm not sure yet,' I answered.

'You'll have to let me know,' he said, getting up and walking over. 'I've got a few friends in there, I could ask 'em to look out for him if you want; make sure he dun't have no trouble from anybody.'

I grinned. Donny'd never even met my brother; Leon didn't mean a thing to him. And yet, he was gonna go out of his way to take care of him – and it was all cos of me; cos I was one of the boys.

'Thanks,' I said, still grinning. 'I'll see you later.'

But as I turned to go, Donny spoke to me again. 'You alright about Thursday night?' he said softly.

'Sure,' I said, and I was surprised how much it sounded like I meant it.

'Sound. You're a proper good lad.' He nodded, then opened a drawer next to him and got something out. 'Maybe you oughta take this though, just in case.'

I looked at his hand and saw he was holding a knife. The handle was black with a shiny metal bit at the end, and a black leather cover was fastened round the blade.

'I ... err ...' My eyes went back to his face. But how could I tell him I wasn't sure about it, after what he'd just said about Leon?

'Calm down – it's not like I'm expectin' you to use it.' He laughed, then stopped again quickly. 'It's just if you did ever need one, you know, to defend yourself? I wouldn't want to think you were stuck without it.' He moved his hand nearer to mine. 'Go ahead, Mikey; it might save your life sometime.'

I took hold of the knife and put it into my inside pocket without looking at it again.

Donny squeezed my shoulder, and turned away.

He's probably right, I told myself, as I left the café – I won't ever actually use it; it'll just be there as a backup, to scare off anybody who starts. It was the other boys who were gonna be taking care of the proper big stuff, I wasn't even gonna get that involved. Like Shane'd said, it'd all be OK.

And somehow, I managed to keep myself thinking that way for the next three days.

TWELVE

Me and Shane stood well back in the shadows. It was Thursday night and we were standing on one of the side-roads near Frankie's, waiting for the others to show up. It was proper windy and absolutely pissing it down; freezing drops of rain ran down my face and the back of my neck, and the old trainers I was wearing felt like they were made of sponge.

Finally, a banged up Rover and an old Astra stopped at the side of the road in front of us. Tyler was driving the Astra and Paulie was next to him in the passenger seat.

Jake got out of the Rover, and as he walked past us he nodded at it. 'You can have that one,' he said.

Shane smiled. 'Cheers mate, you're all heart.'

We'd already decided that Shane would do most of the driving; he knew the area better than me and he'd have more chance of losing anybody who ended up following us. We got in and I lit a fag, probably about my third in the last half hour. Wish it was something stronger, I thought, as I took a long first drag.

Neither of us talked as we drove along. The radio was knackered, so the only noise came from the windscreen wipers as they flew backwards and forwards, fighting to keep the bouncing rain off the glass.

I put my hand into the inside pocket of my jacket. The knife that Donny'd given me a few days earlier felt cold and heavy. We'd all got 'em, and Shane and Paulie had fetched the guns as well. Donny'd said not to use 'em unless Kaler's lot started first though, cos once the guns'd been used, they were easier to trace.

I kept expecting to see blue flashing lights amongst all the orange ones that passed us. But none came, and after about twenty minutes we turned left on to Kaler's road. Paulie and Jake pulled in at one end and we stopped at the other. We could all see the house and the two BMWs parked outside it.

The engine was still switched on, but the bloody heater must've been knackered as well as the radio, and sitting there in piss-wet-through clothes, I started to shiver.

Shane checked the time on his phone and lit a fag.

'How long?' I said.

'Just over five minutes.'

I checked the knife again. If everything went to plan I shouldn't really need it. But I kept on checking it anyway.

After a couple more minutes, Shane stubbed his fag out. 'You ready then, mate?' he said.

I nodded.

Shane stepped on to the road and straightened up, then he turned back round and leaned forward. 'Don't get out unless ya really have to,' he said. 'And for God's sake, don't forget your seatbelt.'

I nodded again, and he closed the door quietly.

Shane walked over to where Paulie and Jake were waiting, then they all disappeared up one of the driveways next door to Kaler's house. I scrambled over into the driver's side and put the seatbelt on straightaway. The windows were starting to mist up, so

I wound mine right down. Then I sat there breathing hard. My trainer tapped quickly against one of the pedals, and sprays of rain from the open window hit the side of my face. The takeaway delivery could come from either direction, and my eyes flicked between the windscreen and the rear view mirror.

When the bottom half of Kaler's driveway suddenly lit up, I twisted my head round to look at it. Their front door was wide open, but I couldn't see anybody about. What were they up to? Did they know we were there?

I was just trying to decide if I oughta do something, when two people appeared in the doorway. One was a lass who'd got her back to the road, and the other was a guy. He put his hand on her backside as he kissed her, then when they'd done, she started to walk away. Just as she got to the top of the drive though, the man's voice echoed round the street. 'Shona,' he shouted, a lot louder than he needed to.

The girl stopped and slowly went back to the door. He said something else to her that I couldn't make out, then she dashed up the drive again, turned, and headed straight towards me.

I slid down in the seat. The last thing I needed was her being able to recognise me. A streetlight shone on her face as she crossed over right in front of me, and it made a big diamante 'S' around her neck sparkle. But her eyes stayed forward, and even when she got into a yellow Mini parked opposite and drove away, she still never noticed me.

Kaler's front garden had been lit up by a security light as she'd left, but when I looked back it'd gone off.

The front door was closed and everything was like it had been before; I breathed out steadily.

Looking straight ahead again, I revved the accelerator gently. It must've been well after eleven by then. I pushed the clutch down, eased the gear stick into first, then slipped it out again. My eyes went back into a rhythm; up to the mirror, then down to the windscreen.

Somehow, the grip I had on the steering wheel got even tighter as the small white delivery van eventually came into sight. It was coming towards me from the front, and I watched it indicate, slow down and park-up in the space that the Mini'd just left. A bloke got out and crossed over. He checked the number of the house, then went down the path and knocked on the door. The security light turned itself on again.

Putting the car back into gear, I waited. After about ten seconds, the front door swung opened and a tall guy stood there looking down at the delivery bloke. There was no need to wait any longer, so I didn't.

I switched the headlights on, released the handbrake and pushed the accelerator down to the floor. There were about fifty yards between me and the BMW, and the engine roared like a jet plane. But I kept my eye on the clock; they'd told me not to hit it at any more than thirty – I mean, I didn't want to kill myself. But even at that speed, you wouldn't believe what it felt like to go crashing smack bang into the back of a parked car.

My head jerked forward and I felt the muscles, or tendons, or whatever they are in the back of your neck, get stretched like a catapult. The seatbelt dug into my chest hard, but it stopped my head hitting the wheel, and I managed to get myself together fairly quickly.

The engine'd cut out, but it started up again straight away, thank God. Donny'd said to get both cars away if we could, so I put it in reverse, drove back about twenty yards, and watched. There was a lot of shouting at first, then the guy who'd answered the door came sprinting up the path. When he got to the top he hesitated for a second, gawping at the crushed up mess that used to be the boot of his car.

Jake came out from behind him, I saw his arm swing forward and the bloke never knew what hit him; he went down hard and laid there with his legs sort of screwed up underneath him. Jake backed off up the drive again.

In the time it took me to blink, another four guys'd left the house and appeared on the road. Four? There weren't supposed to be that many.

Shane, Paulie and Jake all came into view and took one each. The fourth guy set off towards me with something in his hand, but I'd no idea what.

It all happened right fast. I grabbed hold of the knife with one hand and reached out towards the handle on the inside of the door with the other. But then I remembered what Shane'd said and I stopped. I looked round, not sure what to do next.

And then I saw 'em. In the glow of the streetlight, I saw that the guy who was racing up to me was wearing the same bright orange and black trainers he'd been wearing the day Rocco got cut up.

'You bastard,' I shouted, remembering how he'd slammed Rocco's head into the pavement, and something inside my head just blew. I put my foot down, spun the wheel round and went up onto the kerb. He had nowhere to go, and all he could do was stare at me as I hit him straight on. There was this privet hedge thing behind him, and I heard a low thud as both the guy and the front of the car went through it. Cos of the dark, I couldn't make out exactly where he ended up. There was an outline of something laying on the grass in the garden, and I guessed it was probably him, but I wasn't sure.

The engine hadn't stalled this time, and I reversed out on to the road quickly.

I glanced back to where the others had been, but now they were nowhere in sight. My eyes shot across to the Astra just as the backdoors banged shut. Had Shane got in with them? I didn't think he would've, but I couldn't see him anywhere. Then the Astra screeched away, and I had to decide whether or not to follow it.

Time was running out; if any of the neighbours'd phoned the cops they'd be here any second, and I half expected that guy to come running out of the garden after me. I had one last desperate look round; for God's sake, where was he?

But at that minute, the passenger side door flew open, and Shane fell into the car.

There was no time to swap seats, so we just had to take a chance. The wheels spun madly at first, but then they got a grip on the tarmac and we were off. We didn't have any headlights on cos obviously they were all smashed in, and it was a bit dodgy at times trying to make the road out. But I managed to get us the half mile or so to the waste ground where we were meeting the others.

When I stopped the car, I noticed Shane'd slipped down in the seat and his eyes were closed.

'Shane? You alright?' I said.

'I'm OK,' he said slowly, but his eyes stayed shut.

'Come on.' My voice got louder, 'Shane, come on. We gotta get out of here.'

He didn't answer me this time though, so I got out and went round to his side of the car. I opened the door, and as the little light thing came on, I saw that mixed in with the rain that was running down his face from his hair, there were streams of blood.

I grabbed Shane's jacket and pulled him onto his feet. Jake must've seen what was happening, cos he came over, and between us we helped Shane across to the Astra and onto the back seat.

Then Jake dowsed the Rover in petrol and torched it.

Tyler set off driving with us all in the Astra, and Paulie phoned Donny. I sat squashed up in the back and tried to dry Shane's face with my jacket. It was too dark to see exactly where it was coming from, but every time we went past a streetlight it looked like he was covered in more watery blood than he had been before. He still hadn't opened his eyes, and when I felt his breathing getting deeper and slower, I reached out and shook him. 'Shane, wake up! Open your eyes.'

'OK, OK,' he groaned, and slowly, it seemed like he was just about managing to focus on me.

Paulie finished the call to Donny and looked round

from the front seat. 'What's up wi' him?'

'It's his head, it's bleedin',' I answered. 'I think he just went unconscious.'

'I didn't see him bang it or owt,' Jake said.

Paulie turned to face forward again. 'Don't worry about it. We'll sort him out when we get to our lass's; he'll be OK.'

I wasn't so sure, he still looked pretty out of it to me. I wiped his face again. Come on, mate, I thought; stay with it.

The car threw us around and Shane's head rocked from side to side for a while. But when we finally pulled up outside a row of small, newish houses, he lifted it up off the back of the seat, leaned forward and looked out of the window. The bleeding had stopped, and his eyes were like normal again.

Although I had to give him a bit of a hand getting out of the car, he made it along the path and into the house on his own. I watched as he went upstairs to clean himself up, and the relief rushed right through me. I don't think I could've coped with the ambulance and hospital thing all over again.

After we'd all got changed and put everything we'd been wearing in the Astra, Jake drove it away and got rid of it. There was some girl hanging around who was friendly with Tyler, and Paulie and Shane gave her the guns; it'd been arranged that she was gonna look after 'em.

The others all went into the living room then, but I hung back. When we were on our own, I said to Shane, 'How'd you do that?'

'One of 'em must've had a knife,' he said. 'I took a couple of punches an' all, but I don't think it were them that cut me. There was that much happening, I'm not right sure, but it looks like it were a blade. Don't know why I blacked out though, it's hardly owt.'

'So, what happened then – with them?' I asked.

Shane's eyes flickered. 'I got one of 'em, but only on his arm I think. Paulie had a proper go with one of the others, and that first guy that came up the path? He were in a right mess.' He looked at me and smiled. 'You did your bit though, didn't ya? Rammin' that guy into that hedge?'

I smiled back at Shane, but my stomach was spinning.

Somehow, at the time, it'd been like watching it all on telly or playing it on a game. But listening to what Shane'd just said, and looking at the dry blood in his hair, made me realise how real it was; we'd actually done all that.

'C'mon you two,' Paulie shouted to us from the living room. 'Stop gossipin' like a pair of old women and get in here – we've got some celebrating to do.'

We went through as Paulie's girlfriend handed bottles of Stella out. Paulie took the lid off one and lounged across the settee, grinning. 'Not a bad night's work, eh, lads? That first un got the shock of his bloody life – one minute he were worryin' about his car, the next he'd got a gobful of pavement. An' them others were a right load of retards an' all; it took 'em about an hour to work out what were happenin'.' He pulled his girlfriend on to the settee next to him and put his arm round her. 'Jesus, I thought they'd proper clocked us at first though when that door opened. Thank God it were only that lass.' He sniggered. 'D'ya think that 'S' round her neck stood for 'slag' or 'slapper'?'

Tyler laughed like a Halloween skeleton, then Jake came back in and they all started banging on about what they'd done. Their stories got louder and more full of shit as it got later, and all I wanted to do was get back to the home.

When I thought I'd stayed as long as I needed to, I leaned over and told Shane I was gonna chip. He nodded and we both slipped out. The others probably didn't even notice we'd gone, they were so busy chattin'.

I phoned Corky, and about a quarter of an hour later his taxi dropped us off back near Holly House. I let Shane go in first, then I snuck round to the empty house next door. It'd got this broken down old shed in the back garden, and I hid the knife just inside it. It was still throwing it down with rain and my clothes got soaked – again. I smoked a fag, waited as long as I could, then went in.

When I eventually made it upstairs after the usual row with the night staff, Shane was waiting for me outside Jasmine's room.

'Can ya see any blood on me?' he said quietly.

His hair was wet where he'd washed it, and I checked all round his face and head. 'Nah, you're alright.'

He lowered his voice even more. 'If Jasmine says owt about tonight, we played snooker then went to

Previews, OK?'

'Yeah, sure,' I said.

'Cheers, mate.' Shane smiled. 'And if I don't see ya in the mornin', I hope it goes OK.'

'Thanks,' I nodded, and I started to go towards my bedroom door.

'Hey, Mikey.' Shane's whisper made me stop and look at him again. 'Make sure ya don't go leaving that blade in ya pocket. If they find it, you'll not just be visitin' him, you'll end up sharin' a cell wi' him.'

I laughed. 'It's already sorted, mate. Ta though.'

After a couple of seconds I turned away and went to bed.

So that was tonight over with, and at least we were all still alive and not banged up; for now, anyway. So that was a result.

I knew it wasn't the end of it; they were probably already thinking about what they could do to get us back. But that was all in the future – and hopefully, long enough in the future to give me a bit of time, cos all I wanted to concentrate on now, was wondering what tomorrow'd bring.

THIRTEEN

Molly was late. It was ten past nine and she hadn't even showed up yet. I stood next to the front window in the lounge and stared out – just like I had been doing for the last half hour.

'Still no sign?' Ruth said, as she walked into the room.

I glared at her. Did she think I'd be standing there like some kind of an idiot if Molly was waiting outside?

She obviously realised I was getting proper wound up and she stopped, deciding not to come any closer.

'I'll go and give her a ring,' she said, turning round. 'I'm sure she'll be on her way.'

I looked back out of the window. If she doesn't come, I swear down I'm gonna smash this whole place up. Just you watch. Just you see if I don't …

I tapped my fingers on the windowsill and didn't blink for ages. Useless. Why were they all so bleeding useless? I mean what was wrong with 'em? All she had to do was get here at nine like she's said. Stupid slag, wait 'til I –

Molly's car pulled up outside the window. I swirled round, and five seconds later I was sitting in the passenger seat next to her.

'I'm sorry, I'm sorry,' she said, before I had chance to say anything. 'There was an accident, the road was closed; I had to go about a million miles out of my way to get back round to Chapel Cross. We're still alright for time though, I've allowed plenty, so don't worry.'

I took a big breath in and managed to keep my gob shut. It wasn't easy though, the thought of her not turning up, the thought of me not getting to see him; it made me wanna fight the world.

But I needed to chill. I needed to calm myself down and keep everybody on my side.

After a while, I'd settled down enough to talk to her, and I asked her what time we'd got to be there for.

'Ten thirty,' she said. 'We've got a full hour with him.'

'Have you seen him?' I asked her.

'Yes.' She nodded. 'It was me and one of my colleagues who went up to tell him about you last week.'

'What's he look like?'

'Very much like you actually, it's easy to tell you're brothers.'

I smiled; I'd been hoping we looked like each other. Then I wondered if we were alike in any other ways. 'Do you know what he's in for?' I asked.

'Why don't you wait and ask him yourself?' Molly said.

I was quiet for ages then. I had some idea of how he looked now, and I pictured an older version of me in my head. He was laughing, talking to me, being nice to me. I fidgeted about in the seat, crossed my legs, then uncrossed 'em and stretched 'em out. I felt so excited I couldn't keep still – you know how you do when you're a kid and you're going away on holiday or something like that?

But then the car radio jolted me right out of my little

dream.

'It's Radio Sheffield news.' The man's voice was loud and cheerful. *'Our main story this morning is that one man's dead, and three more have been left injured after they were the victims of a knife attack in Sheffield. The assault occurred in the Northwood area of the city at around eleven o'clock last night, and police are asking anyone who witnessed the incident, or who may have any information, to come forward immediately. We'll bring you more on this story as details come in.'*

One dead? Jesus, that wasn't supposed to happen.

My back went rigid. Which one was it?

Could it be him I hit with the car? I hadn't been going fast, but I suppose you don't have to be. It all went through my head again; the kerb, the privet, the dull thud. Had he moved afterwards? I wasn't sure. Perhaps he hadn't.

I started to burn up. I reached out and opened the window as far as it'd go.

Molly looked over. 'You've gone pale,' she said. 'Are you feeling travel sick?'

I didn't answer. Instead, I moved closer to the window. It was cos of what he did to Rocco; I'd have never done it otherwise. Even though he'd been running towards me, I'd have come up with something else. I wouldn't have hurt him that bad on purpose. My teeth bit into the inside of my bottom lip so hard, the taste of blood spread all around my mouth. I hadn't meant to, it'd just happened; I never wanted to ...

But you don't even know you have, I told myself quickly. It might not even be him. If you think about it, it's a lot more likely to be one of the others – like that one Jake got first.

Knowing any of 'em was dead was enough to make me feel shaky, but I just had to believe it wasn't cos of me.

I clung on to that thought with everything I'd got, and that, together with the cold air on my face, eventually meant I relaxed enough to keep it together.

What they'd said about witnesses though, that still bugged me. There weren't any, I was pretty sure about that. Even if any of the neighbours'd been looking out of their windows, all they would've seen were some kids dressed in black. Hats on, hoods up, faces covered. There was no way they'd be able to identify us.

And the Kalers wouldn't be talking to the cops either, would they? They'd be too busy deciding how to settle it their own way.

We'll be OK, I thought. Just don't let it get to you. Don't even think about it, not now. Don't let it spoil what's happening now.

And I was just doing my best to put it out of my mind, when we saw a blue and white sign on our right, that said *Dalton Young Offenders' Institute*.

Everything about the prison was grey; the buildings, the fences, the razor wire – and today, even the sky. Molly had booked it as a professionals' visit, so after we'd put our phones and everything into a locker, we went and sat in this waiting room. I looked at the badges on the other people who were there, most of 'em worked for the Youth Offending Service and they were all holding diaries or files.

I was only a few minutes away from seeing him now, and for the millionth time I thought about what I ought to say to him when I did. What would he say to me? What if he didn't like me?

Molly peered across. 'Don't worry, you'll be fine. Just take things slowly.'

Don't worry? I couldn't remember what it was like to not worry.

A guy came in then, and he told us they were ready. We had to go back outside, wait for a couple of grey metal gates to be unlocked, then queue up to show our identification. Two more locked doors later, and we walked into a big room.

There were about twenty small round tables, and each table had three or four soft chairs surrounding it. The kids who were being visited were already sitting there, one to a table.

My eyes darted around everywhere trying to pick Leon out, but I couldn't. I turned to Molly and she pointed towards a lad at the back of the room. He'd already seen us, and he was smiling.

Molly walked in front of me, and as we got nearer, Leon stood up. He was like me; taller, broader and obviously older, but so much like me. I stopped and looked at him. He paused for just a second, then he stepped over and put his arms round me.

I almost cried. I swear down, you just don't know how it felt. In all my life, it was the first time I'd had a hug from anybody who was family. He held me proper tight, and I'd never felt so safe.

As I stood there, with my head resting against his

shoulder, all I could hear was his heart beating; it was like it was the only sound in the world.

When he did eventually back off a bit, he wiped his eyes and laughed. 'Hey little bro', you're gonna think I'm a right wuss.'

I smiled. It was pointless trying to talk; I knew I wouldn't be able to get any words out.

'Come and sit down,' he said, then he nodded at Molly. 'It's good to see you again. Thanks for bringin' him up.'

'It's my pleasure,' Molly said.

Leon sat down next to me. 'So what you been up to then?'

Christ, if only you knew …

But I put all that to the back of my mind. 'Not much,' I managed.

I tried to think of something else to say then, but it was no good; I just couldn't keep it all in any longer.

'I … I can't believe I'm finally with you,' I blurted out, and I put my head down quickly so they wouldn't be able to see how hard I was trying to hold the tears back.

Leon put his hand on my shoulder. 'It's OK. I know you've been on your own for a long time, Mikey. I know it must have been really crap for you as well, but we've got each other now, haven't we?' He squeezed the top of my arm a bit. 'And it's not like I'm gonna be running off anywhere soon, is it?'

I glanced back up at him and he was smiling at me. My mouth broke into a grin without me even thinking about it, and I didn't care if he saw the tears anymore, cos he understood.

He let me just sit there for a bit 'til I could manage to talk again, and when I did, I asked him one of my biggest questions. 'Can you remember being with our mum?'

He shook his head. 'I were only a few months old when I got put into care. I haven't seen her since.'

'Have you ever tried to find her?'

'No. She knew what she were doin'. His big smiley eyes suddenly turned cold. 'She had her chance and she decided she didn't want me – why should I make the effort?'

A shiver shot down the back of my neck and he noticed.

'I'm well pleased you made the effort though, mate. Finding out I'd got you was the best news I've ever had.' He laughed and I relaxed again; maybe there were just some subjects that we oughta stay away from?

We talked non-stop about everything else though then. He asked me about where I was living and about school and stuff like that. I was really vague when he mentioned school, and thankfully Molly didn't grass me up. I found out a bit about where he'd stayed when he was younger, and I went on about all the foster carers I'd had. Then he told me he'd been living with his girlfriend in Leeds before he got banged up. She was called Chrissy, and he said that next time I came he'd show me a photo of her. I gave him my mobile number as well, and he promised to phone me whenever he could.

Before we knew it, a voice on this tannoy thing told

us we'd only got a couple of minutes left.

'It's time already?' Leon said to Molly.

'Almost,' she answered.

Right, I thought, if you wanna know, you've gotta ask him now. You can't put it off any longer.

I moved both my hands down on to the seat of my chair and gripped the edge. I couldn't look at him, so I put my head down as well, then I said, 'How come you ended up in here?'

He didn't say anything for a few seconds, and I wanted to lift my head back up so I could see his face, but I didn't.

Eventually, I heard him take a deep breath and he said, 'Because I was an idiot, Mikey, that's why. I wanted to be hard and tough, and I always had somethin' to prove.' He paused, and his voice went right quiet. 'It were GBH this time, with a few other things as well. I'd been havin' some trouble with a guy for ages, it's a long story. But I've got a lot of previous an' all from when I was younger; I've been in and out of these kinda places since I were your age.'

GBH, that was pretty serious, wasn't it?

'So, how long did you get?' I asked him.

'Four,' he said. Then he added quickly, 'But I should only have to do two, which means I've got just under a year left.'

It was longer than I'd hoped, but I suppose it could've been worse.

People were starting to leave. 'Sorry, it's time for us to go,' Molly said.

We stood up and Leon put his arm round my

shoulder. 'You take good care of yourself, won't ya?'

I nodded.

'And you'll come again?'

'Course,' I said, like he'd just asked the dumbest question ever.

He laughed and ruffled my hair. 'You're a real cool kid,' he said. 'I'm proud of ya.'

I couldn't say anything else then; my voice'd gone again.

Leon patted my back a couple of times and I walked away. When we got to the door, I stopped and turned round. He was still watching us and he winked and nodded. I almost went running back to him, but Molly guided me towards the door and followed me out.

I was gutted as we walked back to the car. I mean he was great, wasn't he? He was proper sound; I couldn't have wished for anybody better. But after all these years of being apart, an hour just wasn't enough. I wanted to stay with him forever.

Gradually though, I began to brighten up and I started to focus on everything that'd gone right.

'How do you feel?' Molly said after we'd been driving a bit.

'OK. Tired though,' I answered, which was the truth.

'These things can be very emotional, I'm not surprised you're feeling a little drained.'

'Have we got the same dad, me and Leon?' I asked her.

I'd always just thought we wouldn't have, but after seeing him, I couldn't help wondering if we might.

'I don't know, love,' Molly said. 'There's no mention of either of your fathers in our files.'

Oh well, that didn't really matter anyway, did it? I didn't need a dad, 'specially not now I'd got my brother. And I leaned my head back, closed my eyes, and in my mind I went back over everything he'd said and done during the time I'd been with him.

FOURTEEN

I didn't really see anybody when I first got back to Holly House. Ruth was waiting to find out how it'd gone, and you could see she really was pleased when I told her it'd been good. I don't know if she was happy cos of how much it meant to me, or if she was just relieved that she didn't have to deal with me kicking off – which I probably would've done if he'd been a tosser.

Anyway, I didn't tell her that much, cos I couldn't wait to get upstairs and be on my own for a bit. I needed some time. I needed to just be able to think about Leon; think about what it could all lead to.

And what I thought was this: he's got about a year left inside, right? I'll have finished school by then – like officially finished school – and I'll be sixteen. As it is now, even if he came out next week there's a good chance they'd never let me stay with him. Social Services would do assessments, see, and a twenty year old with a chaotic background and convictions for violent crime, probably wouldn't come out as an ideal carer. He's hardly right up there with Mary Poppins, is he?

But in a year's time though, if I just disappear from here and go and live with him, nobody'll really care – I mean let's face it, I'll be saving Mr and Mrs Taxpayer a fortune. Everybody'll be a winner.

Oh I know. I know I'm rushing in, counting my chickens and running before I can walk, but what else do you expect? This was like the best thing that'd happened to me, ever.

Obviously there was a chance he wouldn't actually go for it. But today'd been so cool, he was so buzzin' about it all; I was just sure he'd want me.

***

I dropped off into a deep sleep after a bit. Like I'd said to Molly, I was proper knackered after it all, and Shane must've been knocking on my bedroom door for ages before he finally woke me up.

I opened the door to find him beaming at me. 'So what's ya big brother like then?' he asked, as he walked past and sat on the bed.

'OK,' I said.

He frowned. 'Only OK?'

'Nah. He's right sound,' I answered, smiling.

'Said he would be, didn't I?'

I nodded, and my cheeks started to ache cos the smile got so big.

'You seen the news?' Shane asked a few seconds later.

'I heard it on the radio this morning. It said one of 'em were dead.' Thinking about it all again soon took the smile off my face, and I felt my elbows start digging into my sides.

'Yeah, that one that Jake got first. He were a right dickhead; I bet even Kaler's glad to have got rid of him.'

So it wasn't the guy I'd hit with the car, then. My shoulders loosened up; I'd got away with it, this time.

'Has anybody been round or owt?' I said.

'Nah. The coppers are concentrating on Northwood for now. They won't find owt out about us though; I swear down, we're well in the clear. All the evidence went up in flames, and even if they do start to think it were us, I can't see any of Kaler's lot talkin', can you?'

'Suppose not,' I said.

But to be honest, it wasn't their words that were bothering me – it was what they'd do if they did find out who it was that made my stomach feel like a washing machine with cement going round inside it.

'We've gotta watch ourselves of course, just like last time,' Shane said. 'But if owt does happen, it won't be yet; they'll let things cool off first.'

'Right.' I took a deep breath and nodded.

'Anyway, Donny's well pleased. He's slipped us all an extra few quid. Here.'

Shane reached into his jeans' pocket and brought out a load of notes, he peeled off five twenties and held 'em out to me.

I hesitated, then eventually took 'em.

'Ta,' I said quietly, as I looked down at the notes. For some reason, the money made me feel a bit strange, you know, sort of uneasy?

'Don't spend it all at once,' Shane said, as he got up and went towards the door. 'You out tonight?'

'Yeah, I'll be there later.'

'OK, see ya then.'

***

We should've really gone straight to Previews that night – it was the weekend and there'd have been plenty of business. But when I met Shane he told me he'd already had a good day, and he asked me if I wanted to go round to Rocco's for a bit instead. Donny knew I wouldn't be doing much anyway cos of going to see Leon, so I decided it'd be OK.

I'd been to Rocco's flat a few times before. It was usually a bit of a tip, with clothes and DVDs and stuff all over the place. But it always made me smile as well – cos Rocco had a thing about Scooby Doo. There were pictures of that bloody dog everywhere, and then there were things like Scooby Doo cups and Scooby Doo ashtrays, even a Scooby Doo clock … you get the picture? It really was proper funny.

Rocco was tons better than he'd been at The Forge that night. He was smiling and laughing and lively again, and after he'd dished some cans out, he must've asked us a million questions about what'd happened with the Kalers. Shane told him more or less everything that'd gone on, and Rocco sat there listening like a kid at story time, with his face changing between grins and frowns depending on which bit Shane was describing.

After that we played this new game on his Xbox, and Rocco put some tunes on. We talked about normal stuff and it was cool.

At one bit, Rocco said, 'Oooh, that lass from downstairs came up yesterday. You know the one with red hair and legs like Barbie? She were askin' about you.' He nodded at Shane. 'I reckon you could be in there, mate.'

I smiled. 'He's already been in there, mate.'

Shane laughed, and Rocco's mouth dropped open for a second before he said, 'How come I never knew?'

Shane winked at him. 'I can't tell ya about 'em all, sunshine, can I? There'd be no time left to talk about owt else. It were only once anyway.'

Rocco tutted. 'When?'

'Oh I don't know, a couple of months ago maybe. Why?'

'You still interested?' Rocco said.

'Nah,' Shane shook his head, then he looked at him and grinned. 'Aah, you are though, aren't ya?'

Rocco smirked. 'Well I might be, if you're not bothered anymore. But why'd ya dump her so quick though? Is there summat wrong with her?'

'She's alright,' Shane said. 'It's just that …'

'It's just that he's in lurve,' I said. 'Can't you hear the sound of female hearts breakin' all over Chapel Cross? Shane's turned into a one girl guy.'

'No way!' Rocco was good at being gobsmacked. 'Who's is she?'

'Just somebody I know.' Shane swapped the Xbox game over and started playing again.

'She any good?' Rocco asked, grinning.

'Mind your own bloody business,' Shane said, without taking his eyes off the telly.

Me and Rocco looked at each other, smiled and raised our eyebrows. Usually, you couldn't shut him up when he was telling you about the lasses he'd been with. So Shane keeping quiet about Jasmine was a right bloody miracle.

We had a few more drinks then went. It was a long time since we'd just messed around like that, and with the Kaler thing out of the way for now, and my first visit to Leon over with, I felt better than I had for ages.

***

Every time my phone rang for the next two weeks I hoped it was Leon, but it wasn't. If I'm honest, I started to get a bit worried. Maybe he wasn't as keen as I thought? Maybe he'd been thinking about it all and decided he was better off without a kid brother tagging along? Maybe he didn't really like me?

Molly was slow timing about arranging another visit, and whenever I tried to ring her I had to leave a message, cos predictably, she wasn't there. I really started to believe that what'd happened with Leon was some sort of dream, and now I'd woken up, it was all just words and pictures in my head that'd never actually existed in the proper world.

But then, one afternoon when I was in my bedroom, all those dreamy words and pictures got real again.

I nearly didn't answer my phone, cos the number that showed up wasn't another mobile and wasn't from round here. Even when he asked if it was me, I still didn't cotton on who was calling, and I was cagey right up until he told me who it was.

But once I knew it was Leon, I was buzzin'.

'How are you?' I said.

'I'm OK, how about you?'

'Yeah, fine.'

'I'm sorry I haven't been able to phone sooner, mate, but it's not always easy. I didn't really expect ya to answer now; I thought you'd still be in school. But it were the only chance I'd got. What time did ya finish?'

I cringed, and looked down at my phone. It was only half two, I couldn't say I'd already left.

'Oh, erm, I haven't been in ... it's a teacher training day.'

I chewed hard on one of my finger nails; it didn't really feel right lying to him, but then again, telling him the truth wasn't really an option, was it?

'I've just phoned Chrissy and told her all about ya,' Leon carried on. 'She's really cool; you'll like her. D'ya know when you'll be able to get back up here?'

'Nah, they've not sorted it out yet. But when we got back last time, Molly said she'd get something set up within about a month – so it shouldn't be too long. I'll keep buggin' her and I'll write and let you know as soon as she gets back to me.'

'Sound. You'll need to put my prison number and C Wing on the envelope. Listen, I've gotta go cos we don't get much time, but I'll phone again when I can, OK?'

'Oh, alright. See you,' I said slowly.

'You be a good lad, yeah?'

'Yeah.'

And that was it. About a minute if that, and he had to hang up.

But at least he'd phoned in the first place. He cared enough about me to get in touch – and that was more than anybody else'd ever done.

I went outside and sat on the wall to smoke a fag.

'Be a good lad,' that's what he'd said. But how could I now? I'd moved on from being a good lad, hadn't I?

I looked down at the end of my fag and watched as it slowly burned away and the ash fell on the floor. I really am sorry big bro', but I just can't go back to school, not now. The idea of sitting there, trying to learn about Shakespeare and algebra and God, having to get up at the crack of dawn, staying in at night to do homework, not being able to have a fag whenever I wanted ... wearing uniform! Nah, I shuddered. It was just never gonna happen; I wouldn't be able to hold it all together.

There was the money I'd be losing out on as well. I was used to having it now, used to having all the stuff it bought. There's no way I'd be able to go back to living off what the home gave me.

And apart from all that, there was Donny. I mean it's just not as easy as walking in there one day, handing the knife and the gear back over, and saying, *'Ta for all your help, Donny. It's been great workin' for ya and finding out all about sellin' illegal drugs. And I was more than happy to help out with all that Kaler business, you know where one of 'em ended up gettin' murdered? But now I'm gonna call it a day if that's OK with you? I thought I'd go back to school and be a good boy, get some qualifications and a job? So cheerio then.'*

No. I knew way too much about Donny and his empire. Me, in the area, but not actually being part of things anymore was far too risky for him; he needed to keep me close for now.

That doesn't mean I'm stuck here forever though, I told myself. If I do go and live with Leon, then I'll be going to another city, and that'll be OK won't it? None of Donny's rivals'll be around to try and get at me, and the cops won't know where I've gone. Nobody'll be so bothered about me they'll track me down to Leeds.

Getting out of Sheffield was the only way of getting out of the life, but until Leon was released, there was nowhere out of the city I could go to.

So it all came down to waiting again. And what I decided to do while I was waiting, was do enough to keep Donny sweet, but not get in too deep if I could help it. Keep being vague about school when I talked to Leon, and try to save a bit of cash up – having a few quid behind me was never gonna be a bad thing, was it? Leon'll probably not have much when he gets out, so it'll be a big help there.

If he has me.

I lit another fag. That was a good thing he'd said though, wasn't it, about me liking Chrissy? That sort of made me think I'd definitely be meeting her at some point and he hoped we'd get on well. I wondered what she was like. I could do without her being some hard faced cow. I mean it was one thing convincing Leon he wanted his long lost little brother to come and live with him, but what was in it for her? Why should she let some kid who she'd never met before come and move in with 'em?

Mmm, I might have to work on that one. I suppose

I'll have to make it clear that I can look after myself and that I won't get in their way or be any trouble or anything. And like I said, I should have a fair bit of money by then, so I'll be able to pay my own way.

I stopped thinking about it all then, cos I caught sight of Jasmine walking along the road towards me. She was on her way back from school and she looked right young in her uniform; you would've never known she was going on for sixteen.

She stopped and smiled when she got to me.

'Good day?' I asked her.

'Not bad. I had a nightmare in science though; we were doing this experiment and mine went wrong, I ended up setting this rubber tube thing on fire and it all melted. Teacher went on a right rampage. She was trying to clean it up and it was all like gooey and stringy and sticking to everything it touched.'

Jasmine started to giggle and I smiled as well.

When she finally stopped, she said, 'Is Shane inside?'

'Err, I think he's out.' I wasn't gonna tell her where or anything – I didn't know how much she knew.

'Oh. I hope he's not gonna be too long. Do you know where he's gone?'

I needed to change the subject, but the best thing I could come up with was, 'Nah, but hey, did you know we've got a new whizz-bangin' telly? It got delivered today; it's bloody massive.'

'Oh, that's awesome. They were on about EastEnders at school today; they were saying it's right good at the minute, cos ...'

Jasmine chatted on about that dumb soap for the next two minutes, and I tried hard to pretend I was listening. She talked about this and that character and what they were up to and I nodded and raised my eyebrows in the right places – I think.

Then I noticed that all the time, her fingers were messing around with a gold necklace I'd never seen before. I looked at it more carefully and noticed it was made up of tiny heart-shaped links all joined together. No guessing where that'd come from.

Eventually, she realised I was staring at it, and she stopped talking and looked at me.

'Sorry, I were just thinking that's a really nice chain,' I said.

Her cheeks went pink and she looked away. 'Yeah, it's lovely isn't it? Shane bought it for me.'

At that minute, we heard the shrieking voices of the freaky twins and they appeared from inside Holly House. As soon as Jasmine saw 'em she tucked the necklace back inside her shirt, but it was too late. The fattest one'd already seen it, and she came racing up to us like a footie player going up to the referee when he's just had a goal disallowed.

'Ooooh, what's that? Let me look,' she screeched.

'It's nothin',' Jasmine said, and she turned to walk away.

But freaky grabbed her arm. 'Oh, come on. I only wanna look at it; I won't do owt.'

Jasmine stared at me, her eyes were big and scared.

'It's got nothin' to do with you,' I said. 'Leave her alone.'

'What's up with ya both? I just wanna see it …' She put her hand up to Jasmine's neck and started grabbing at the chain.

Jasmine stepped back and made a big effort to yank her arm free, but she was up against somebody who was taller and stronger and heavier, and who had no intention of letting go.

I slipped down off the wall. 'Take your fuckin' hands off her now,' I said. 'Or I'll smash your nasty little head in.'

The fat twin stared at me, trying to work out whether I'd really do it.

Then her slightly thinner sister came and stood by her side. 'Come on,' she said. 'It's not worth it; it's probably only a bit of shiny plastic anyway.'

'Yeah,' said the fat one. 'You can keep it.'

But before they walked away, she stopped and glared at Jasmine. 'He might be shaggin' ya and buyin' ya flash presents now,' she hissed. 'But it won't last long. Believe me, our Shaney likes to put it about a bit. You're soon gonna be history, lady.'

And the pair of 'em really did cackle like witches as they stomped off up the road.

Jasmine had tears in her eyes when I looked at her again.

'Hey, don't worry about them,' I said. 'They're as spiteful and stupid as they are ugly.'

Her face broke into a smile for just a second.

'They've got their eye on that chain though,' I went on. 'I wouldn't leave it layin' around anywhere if I were you.'

145

She shook her head. 'I don't ever take it off,' she said.

It was all quiet for a bit then, and I was just wondering what I could say to break the silence, when she looked up at me.

'Is it true – what they said about Shane?'

I looked away and scratched my head. I was no good at all this emotional stuff. I mean what did she want me to say? That Shane loved her more than he'd ever loved anybody else? That actually, she was probably the only person he'd ever loved in his entire life?

I sighed. 'Look, he thinks a right lot about you, that's all I know.'

But it seemed to be enough for Jasmine. She wiped her eyes on the sleeve of her coat and smiled a proper smile. Then, before I knew what was happening, she flung her arms round me so tight I had to step back so I didn't lose my balance.

I looked down as she snuggled her head into my shoulder. 'Thanks,' she said quietly, and she squeezed me even harder.

Without really thinking about it, my hand edged up slowly round her waist. At first, I held it about an inch away from her, but then I closed my eyes and let it rest gently on her back. She was so warm, and even through her coat I could feel her ribs moving as she breathed. Her fingertips pressed lightly on the back of my neck, and my head dropped forward 'til I felt her soft, smooth hair against my cheek. The next breath I took in, was filled with the smell of honey.

Christ, if she'd have been anybody else's

girlfriend…

But you don't do that to a mate, do you? I let go of her and shrugged her arms off me as I stepped away. 'I'll see you later then,' I said.

'Oh, yeah. Thanks again, Mikey.' Jasmine's eyes were dry and bright, and she almost skipped along as she made her way into the house.

I climbed back onto the wall, holding the bricks tight with both hands. The sky'd gone a deep purply colour, and I gazed up at the single star that shone in it.

It's OK, I told myself; it was nothing. A hug from a friend, that's all. I hadn't done anything wrong and it was gonna stay that way. I'd never do it to him – and even if I would, she wouldn't. You only had to look at how she'd cried when the twins'd gone on about Shane seeing other lasses; she needed him to love her more that she needed air.

No, no, it's cool. I didn't know what'd come over me, but it was a one-off. Maybe I just needed a good night out …

I lit yet another fag up, and hoped that this time I'd be able to enjoy it in peace.

FIFTEEN

Molly eventually got off her arse and came round to see me. She told me she'd set up my next visit to see Leon, went on about school for a bit, then left.

But it made me feel a lot better. I wrote a letter to Leon letting him know the date and time just like I'd promised, then I went out to post it.

Rocco was back working with us by then, and once I'd posted the letter I went and met up with him and Shane. The first thing we had to do was go over to the café to pick some stuff up.

Shane went in first, and as I followed him, somebody sprung up off the leather chair. I looked across to see Paulie straightening his jacket. 'Oh, it's just you lot,' he said.

Shane glanced round. 'Where's Donny?'

'Out.' Paulie reached over to get a can of Red Bull off the shelf.

'How long's he gonna be?'

'Ah, well; that all depends, dun't it?'

'On what?'

'On when he manages to drag himself away from this new bird what's got her claws into him.'

Rocco stepped round from behind me. 'I thought he were shaggin' that tall un – that, err …'

'Chloe?' Paulie smirked. 'Oh, no; she's been kicked right into touch by this new one.'

'So who is she then?' Rocco asked.

'Dunno, he's keepin' her well under wraps; wouldn't know her if she came walkin' in here and sat next to me. But she must have summat, I'm tellin' ya, cos Donny ain't stopped smilin' since he met her.' He paused for a second. 'Let's just hope all that smilin' lasts, shall we?' He took a long swig from the can then, before saying, 'Anyway – what d'ya all want?'

'It's OK,' Shane said. 'We'll come back later.'

Paulie put the drink down and stared at us. 'There's no need; I can sort it for ya.'

'But we don't mind, really; we'll call back in a bit.'

Paulie's voice went quiet and slow. 'I said, I'll sort it for ya, and I will. Now.'

Shane gave a sigh that only I could hear, then he went and let Paulie give him some bags, and me and Rocco did the same.

As we opened the door to leave a few minutes later, Paulie picked the TV remote up, and settled himself back down in the chair.

***

It was still quite early and there weren't many calls coming through, so we went to Frankie's, then the off-license, then round to Rocco's for a bit.

The boxes and cans were about empty, when Rocco finished chewing a big gobful of pizza and said, 'Oh, I had the cops round here last night.'

Me and Shane looked at each other and shook our heads.

Then Shane turned to Rocco. 'You could've told us that before we all came round. We've got enough gear on us to get King Kong off his head – what if they come back?'

'Oh yeah,' Rocco said. 'I don't think they will though. They didn't search the flat or owt, they just wanted to ask me about when I got jumped. They said summat about another recent incident, and that it were just routine. They wanted to know if I could remember owt I hadn't told 'em before.'

'And could ya?' Shane asked, only half joking.

'No way,' Rocco said. 'I ain't told 'em owt, mate.'

'That day, when it happened, what did you have on you?' I said to Rocco.

'Not that much. The guy'd took all the charlie, hadn't he? And I got away with tellin' 'em the weed I had was all for me.'

Well that sounded believable.

'Did they say what incident?' Shane asked him.

'Nah.' Rocco bit into the last piece of pizza. 'They said what I already told ya, then asked me if I could remember owt about the kids what did it. I just acted daft and said my mind were blank. Don't know if they went for it though.'

Me and Shane looked at each other again and tried not to laugh.

'I'm sure you had 'em proper fooled,' Shane said.

I wondered if I ought to be worried about the police coming round to Rocco's. Probably not, I told myself; it probably didn't mean anything at all.

But when I was still thinking about it after a few minutes, I finally said to Shane, 'Do you think it really were just a routine visit?'

'Yeah,' he nodded. 'They didn't bring a warrant, and

they didn't take him down to the station. If they really had summat, they would've done both.'

Well, that sounded believable as well. Just a routine visit – one knife incident followed a few weeks later by another; they had to make some effort to find out if there was any connection, didn't they?

The more cans I drank, the more sure I was that we were right, and by the time the calls started and we had to go to work, I was totally convinced that there was nothing to worry about.

***

The day before I was due to go and see Leon again finally came, but when I walked into Holly House that afternoon, Ruth was on the phone.

'Oh, he's here now,' she said, glancing at me. 'You can speak to him yourself.'

She covered the phone with her hand as she passed it over. 'It's Social Services,' she whispered.

'Yeah?' I said.

The woman's voice was slow and dull. 'Mikey, I'm sorry, but Molly's off ill. She won't be back for at least a week, so we've got to postpone the visit to see your brother that was planned for tomorrow.'

'What?' I heard her words, but my mind wouldn't believe it.

'We've got to postpone the visit to see your brother that was planned for tomorrow.'

'No you … haven't.' Don't swear, I thought, closing my eyes for a second. Keep her sweet.

'I'm afraid we just haven't got anyone else available to take you,' she said.

'What? You mean there's nobody else in that whole building that can do it? What they gonna be doin' all day? Watering their plants? Re-arranging their cushions?'

'It's a matter of priority, Mikey. We all have lots of other commitments, and unfortunately some of them have to take priority over others. I'm not saying the visit won't happen at all, but you'll have to wait until Molly's back.'

I shook my head. When you've been involved with social workers as long as I have, you learn a lot about 'em, right? And one of the things you soon get to know is that when they go off ill, they can be off for months, and sometimes you never see 'em again, ever. Then you have to wait for a new one to be allocated, and when you eventually get somebody, they start telling you that the old one didn't do any of the things they said they were gonna do.

My teeth were clenched tight, but in the calmest voice I could manage, I said, 'Can't you find somebody, anybody who can take me?'

'We have a lot of cases to deal with and very limited resources. I'm sorry, it's just not possible to take you tomorrow, but Molly will be in touch when she's better. Is that alright?'

It was then that I really started to panic; she wasn't gonna change her mind, was she?

'No, it's not alright you stupid bitch. He's my brother, I need to see him. It's your job to sort it out.'

'I know you must be feeling disappointed, Mikey,' she said in exactly the same tone. 'But we have other cases that …'

'Oh for God's sake, just forget it. You're useless, all of you,' I shouted, and I slammed the phone down so hard the plastic cracked and the battery flew out.

I pushed myself back against the wall hard. Somehow I must've slid down it as well, cos I ended up on the floor. Then I got my fags out and lit one – which was an offence usually punishable by death – but Ruth didn't even mention it. Instead, she picked the battery up and put it back in the phone.

I breathed out and looked down. I hated 'em. I hated 'em all. Sitting there in their bloody offices, with their little postcard things up on the wall, you know, the ones that say stuff that's supposed to be funny about how hard they work and how crap their jobs are? Tossers.

I mean, who the hell do they think they are anyway? Making decisions about other people's lives, thinking they know it all, thinking they know what's best for everybody. When actually, they know fuck all.

'Would you like me to speak to them?' Ruth said softly. 'I could try and explain how important it is to you, see if there's any way at all they can find somebody else to take you. I'm not promising, but I'll give it a go if you want me to?'

I sighed; I didn't have a choice, did I? I needed 'em, see. I needed the tossers in the offices because I'd ended up in care, and I wasn't old enough yet to be able to do stuff for myself.

I looked up at Ruth and nodded. 'Yeah,' I said

quietly.

And by some miracle, she did it. She got to talk to one of the managers and laid it on proper thick. She said things like I was, 'an extremely vulnerable young person,' that I'd got, 'significant attachment issues,' and that having contact with Leon was the only way I could, 'maintain any kind of emotional stability'.

I'm not right sure if I liked being talked about like that; but whatever. I could put up with a few white lies if it got me what I wanted – and it did, cos they finally agreed to send a duty worker round to take me.

***

It was the old woman with the Audi who came to pick me up the next morning. She was alright, but she couldn't half talk, and all the way there she gabbed on about a right load of crap. She drove about as fast as a snail with a hang over as well – a sick car like that, and she never once went over sixty. If only I could've got behind that wheel …

We still got there early though, and we had to hang about before they let us in. I couldn't wait to see him up 'til then, but sitting there in that waiting room, I started to get proper nervous again. I got up and walked around a bit, and I started wanting a fag bad.

But they called us in then, thank God, and as soon as I saw Leon, all the nerves went away. He was taller than I'd remembered, and when he smiled, it wasn't just his mouth that looked happy, it was the whole of his face. His eyes got sort of brighter and bigger, and you could tell he really was pleased to see me; you could tell I meant something to him. I liked that, it felt good.

Leon hugged me. 'I'm proper glad you finally got back up here,' he said.

'Yeah, me an' all. Are you alright?'

'Betta now I've seen you.' He smiled and winked at me. 'How's it goin' then?'

'Oh, OK I suppose.' I didn't mean to sound mardy, but being with him again made me realise how much I'd missed him over the last few weeks – and how much I was gonna be missing him again in an hour's time.

He must've known what was up.

'I've been thinkin' about ya a lot while I've been stuck in my pad; wishin' I could see ya more often,' he said. 'That's what I were on about the last time you came, you know, about me bein' an idiot? If I weren't banged up in here we'd be able to see each other a whole lot more, wouldn't we?'

'It's cool.' I made myself smile at him. 'I mean it's betta than never seein' you at all.'

'Yeah, you're right. But I'm still gonna make it up to ya when I get out – just you wait, I'll make up for all that time we lost out on before.'

Oh, I liked the sound of that. That sounded proper good, didn't it? That sounded like he was thinking what I was thinking. I looked up at him and grinned.

'That'll be wicked,' I said.

He showed me a photo then that he'd been holding in his hand. 'This's Chrissy.'

She was about his age. Her hair was this reddish-brown colour and right curly, and she was smiling. She was pretty but not all tarted up; she looked OK.

'She's nice,' I said. 'How long you known her?'

'Since we were kids. We went to the same school – I mean I weren't really there that much, 'specially as we got older – but we always kept in touch. We moved in together about two years ago. She works in a nursery, you know with babies and little kids?'

Leon'd been staring at the photo while he'd been talking, but then he looked back at me. 'She said, next time she visits, if ya want her to, she'll come an' pick you up and bring you with her?'

'Did she?' Jesus, this was turning into one hell of a good day.

'Err, actually I would have to check that.'

Me and Leon turned to look at the social worker. She pushed her hair back behind her ears and carried on.

'I'd have to discuss it with my manager; it's policy, you see? I'm not saying it can't happen, it's just there are guidelines and procedures we have to follow, before we can decide whether to authorize it.'

There you go; tossers in the offices again. Butting in and making everything a million times more complicated than it needed to be. I opened my mouth to tell her exactly where to shove her guidelines and procedures, but Leon put his hand on my arm and shook his head a bit.

'It's OK,' he said to me quietly, then he looked at her again. 'We'd be really grateful if you could try and sort it out. I'll give you Chrissy's number, and she'll tell ya whatever ya need to know.'

'Thank you; that'll be really helpful. Like I say, I'll speak to our manager, then Mikey's usual worker will contact you if she needs any more details.'

She wrote Chrissy's full name and number down in the diary she'd brought in with her, then she kept quiet until it was time for us to go.

I didn't feel too bad when I left him that time – I was sure I'd be seeing him again pretty soon, and everything he'd said about the future was good.

He gave me another hug as we said goodbye, then me and the social worker made our way out.

The last thing I felt like was listening to her voice all the way back to the home; I wanted to be left alone. So as soon as we got into the car, I put my MP3 player on, leaned my head back and closed my eyes – she took the hint.

After a while, I could tell we'd pulled in somewhere, but I knew we hadn't been driving long enough to be back already. I opened my eyes just wide enough to see that we'd stopped at a petrol station, then I shut 'em again quickly.

She called my name a few times but I ignored her, and she eventually fell for it; she believed I really was asleep. She took the keys out of the ignition and got out, leaving me alone in the car. I waited 'til I heard the petrol cap being closed up and her walking away, then I had a look around. I honestly wouldn't have taken anything, but I couldn't help having a look.

There was a few quid in one of the compartments in the dashboard, and the usual de icer and stuff in the glove compartment. On the floor in the back there was one of those Bag for Life things, and I could see some grey coloured files inside it. I wondered if mine was in there – I hadn't seen it for a bit, there might be something new in it.

I looked into the shop part of the petrol station. She was nowhere near the front of the queue, and she'd picked a newspaper up and was busy reading the front page. Turning round again, I tilted the pile of files back a bit so I could see the names on the front. The first one was for some lass – at least I think it was a lass, it was one of those names that could be for either. Then the next was right thin – no way did that one belong to me. But when I got to the third file, I stopped. My heart froze, and my mouth went dry. I glared at it; it couldn't say that, it just couldn't.

But it did. And I read those words over and over again, until I had no other option but to believe 'em; First Name: JASMINE – Family Name: KALER

SIXTEEN

He wasn't at the home when I got back. I thought about phoning him and going to meet him somewhere, but then I decided to wait; it was probably better if we didn't talk about it outside.

I went upstairs and sat on my bed. Then I got up and walked round the room. I had to tell him, didn't I? There wasn't any choice. I mean he could be getting himself into some right trouble; Donny, her family, the other lads. He had to know.

But when I did tell him, I knew he was gonna be proper gutted. I took in a big breath; why couldn't she have been anybody else?

And it was definitely her by the way. I'd checked, just before the social worker got back to the car. I looked inside the file – not to read any of the reports or anything – but I checked her date of birth and current carers, and although I was really hoping it was just a massive coincidence, it wasn't – the file was hers.

I'd left my bedroom door open a bit so I could see the landing, and every time I heard footsteps on the stairs my eyes shot up to see who it was. After about twenty minutes, the person who walked on to the landing, was Shane.

'Hey,' he said. 'How'd it go?'

I looked at him, opened my mouth, then shut it again.

'What's up?' he asked as he walked in.

I went and closed the door behind him, and as I turned back round he spoke to me again.

'Is it ya brother? Is summat up?'

'No, no it's not that – he's fine. It's just … it's just that on the way back, in the car … I saw Jasmine's file …'

Shane tensed up and closed his eyes for a couple of seconds. When he opened 'em again, the look on his face meant I never had to finish that sentence.

It was quiet for what seemed like ages. Shane went over and looked out of the window, then he stared back at me, but he still didn't say anything.

'How long have you known?' I said eventually.

'Since a few weeks after we got together.'

I frowned. 'So why didn't you do something? I mean why you still with her?'

He shrugged. 'I didn't want to do owt.'

That's not exactly the point, I thought; we both know you haven't got a bloody choice.

'When it gets out, the whole world's gonna want to kill you,' I said.

Shane put his hands in his jeans' pockets and turned to look out of the window again. 'Yeah, I know.'

So what was he playing at? Why was he setting himself up for all this bother? I knew she was a real darling, I knew he thought a lot about her, but it just wouldn't ever work.

I wet my lips. 'Mate, you're gonna have to break it up with her; you've just got to.'

He sighed and didn't answer me, then after a few seconds he said, 'Are ya gonna say owt?'

''Course I'm not. But they'll find out eventually, you know they will. What relation is she anyway?'

160

'Kaler's her uncle. Two of the kids we hit that night are her cousins.' He paused for a bit, then he decided to tell me the rest. 'She's got a couple of older brothers that work for Kaler an' all.'

I shook my head. He just couldn't have picked a more dangerous lass to fall for if he'd tried. And it wasn't just her family, was it?

'So what about Donny?' I said.

'Well, he won't exactly be buzzin' about it will he? But he dun't need to know.'

Shane was kidding himself big time. She must've turned him soft or something, cos it was him who'd once told me – *Donny always gets to know stuff.*

It was silent again then for a few minutes. I wondered who else might know apart from me and Shane. And then I wondered if even Jasmine really knew what she'd got herself, and him, into.

I leaned back on the bed. 'How much does she know about you?' I asked.

'She knows what I do – she's not stupid, is she? But she dun't know who for, and she's no idea we had owt to do with the Kaler thing.'

'So what you gonna do?'

Shane turned back to face me. 'I can't finish with her, Mikey, I just can't. I suppose I can try and make it look like I have and hope that works – but if it dun't, then I'm not sure. I'll have to think about it when it happens.'

'*When it happens?* Don't you think it'll be a bit bleedin' late by then?' I spoke louder than I meant to.

But he just smiled at me. 'I'll sort it; don't worry.

And cheers for not sayin' owt.'

He went then, and left me feeling so on edge I couldn't sit still.

I mean for Christ's sake, what was up with him? It was obviously gonna end bad cos there were so many people out there who'd go psycho when they found out, and even I knew it was bound to come out eventually. You just can't keep something like that a secret; not round here.

***

When I met up with Shane the next day he never mentioned what we'd been talking about. In fact, he acted exactly like he always did, and you would've never known there was anything wrong.

We went round to Donny's like usual and they laughed and talked about all the regular stuff. I had to make an effort to join in at first cos I didn't want it to seem like anything was up, but after a while I started to chill as well and it felt OK again.

Donny was in a good mood. That deal he'd been working on in Manchester had gone quiet after Rocco got stabbed, but they'd just been in touch again and it looked like it was all back on. He had to go back over there in a few weeks' time he said, and then it should all be sorted.

I didn't really understand what it all meant, and I asked Shane about it as we walked along afterwards.

'It's summat to do with one of the big hitters over there. Donny's gonna start usin' him to supply us the gear, but it's about back-up an' all. With them on our side, Donny'll be able to start branchin' out a bit, you know, move in on some of the other areas?'

'Like where?' I asked him.

But before he could answer me, his phone rang. Shane sorted out where he'd meet the guy then he put his phone away. He was just about to try and talk to me again when there was another ring. Shane got a different phone out of his pocket that I'd never seen before, and just by the way he answered it, I could tell he was talking to Jasmine.

I wandered off in front of him so he could speak to her in private, but it was only a few seconds later when he caught up with me, and his face was grey.

'Can ya go and meet that guy that just phoned?' he said.

'Yeah, 'course. What's up?'

'Don't ask, mate. Look, I've gotta go; I'll see ya later.'

And he was gone.

What the hell'd she just told him? I hoped he was OK – I mean, I hoped it wasn't her brothers or anything like that. Maybe I should've gone with him? I tried to phone him about five times but he didn't answer. So all I could do was go and meet the guy, and worry about it all for the next few hours.

It was during those next few hours though, that I got a surprise phone call of my own.

'Is that Mikey?' It was a lass's voice that I didn't know.

'Who is it?'

'It's Chrissy – Leon's Chrissy.'

'Oh right. Yeah, it's Mikey.'

'Good. I've just spoken to Leon and he asked me to give you a call. Are you alright?'

'Err, yeah.' She sounded proper nice, sort of friendly and cheerful. 'Thanks for offerin' to take me with you when you go an' see him,' I said. 'Did he tell you about Social Services though?'

'Yes, but don't worry about that. I know it'll hold things up a bit but I'm sure they'll agree to it in the end. They're only doing their jobs, love. They can't just let you go off with somebody without checking them out first; I could be anybody, couldn't I?'

'Suppose so.'

'Anyway, I can't come and see you until the social workers have done their stuff, but Leon wanted me to say hi and he wanted you to have my number – is that OK?'

'Sure, I'm really glad you've phoned. Is he alright, Leon?'

'He's not too bad. I don't know if he's said anything, but he's ever so pleased to have found you, you know. In fact, you're all he talks about now when he phones me up; Mikey this, Mikey that, it's all I hear.' Chrissy laughed, then she was serious again. 'You've made him want to get out more than ever before – and I'm hoping you could even be the one thing that stops him going back in again.'

I smiled a massive smile. Co-ol, I thought, but I didn't really know what to say to her about it. It was quiet for a bit before she spoke again.

'So, I'll let you know when Social Services get in touch, and you can save my number, yeah?'

'Yeah, I'll do it now. Thanks a lot for ringin'.'

'You're welcome – it's been really nice talking to you. And I mean it, Mikey, if you need anything, just give me a call.'

'Yes!' I said out loud after she'd hung up. This just couldn't be going any better. She's proper sound and he's buzzin' about me. If it weren't for the thing with Shane, I wouldn't have had a care in the world …

***

I went straight up to Shane's room when I got back to Holly House. The door was shut, so I knocked and waited.

After he'd asked who it was, he let me in. I looked at him first and felt relieved he was all in one piece, then I noticed Jasmine standing behind him. She kept her head down, but I could tell her eyes were proper red.

'I'll see you later,' Jasmine said in a voice not much louder than a whisper.

'Yeah. I'll have to go out in a bit, but I'll try not to be too long.' Shane kissed her and ran his hand down her back as she went out.

'Sorry, mate – I didn't mean to interrupt anythin',' I said. 'I were just wonderin' if everythin's OK – you know after this mornin'?'

'Oh, you're alright.' Shane turned away and picked his jacket up. 'It weren't really anythin', you know how lasses can be? Everythin's a drama.'

He looked back at me and forced a big smile. 'So how's business been?'

'Quiet.'

'Well, come on then. Let's go an' see if we can earn a few quid to make up for it.'

Shane tried hard to carry on like normal, but there was obviously something wrong, and he was nowhere near as convincing as he'd been that morning at covering it up.

Other people probably wouldn't have picked up on it, like when we hung out with the other lads. Then, he was more or less the good old Shane; laughing and joking around and that. But even as time went on, whenever we were on our own I could tell there was something on his mind.

And it was exactly three weeks later, when I found out what it was.

SEVENTEEN

I was walking past the park when the black BMW pulled in next to me. It'd already gone dark and I was about to get outa there quick. But then the window went down, and I heard Donny's voice. 'Mikey.'

'Yeah?' I stepped over to the car.

'Get in, will you. I wanna ask you somethin'.'

He was smiling and tapping the steering wheel in time to the music playing on Capital FM. But I still hesitated before I went round and got into the passenger seat. He'd never picked me up like that before, and I wondered if I'd done something wrong. My mind went mad trying to think what it could be. But there was nothing; nothing at all.

I put my hands into my pockets and messed about with my keys at one side and my phone at the other. Donny talked about all the regular stuff for a while, then he asked me how Leon was. I answered him carefully, still not really sure what he was up to.

After about fifteen minutes, he parked up on this industrial estate. All the units were closed and their shutters were down. Nobody else was around, and the bit of sky I could see between the buildings was all cloudy and grey.

Donny took his seatbelt off and got a couple of fags out. He passed one over to me and lit it, then he leaned forward and switched the radio off. The hand that was still in my pocked, wrapped slowly round the keys.

'There's a lass that lives where you live,' he said. 'Her name's Jasmine. D'you know her?'

Shit, I know where this's going, I thought. I took a long drag on the cigarette. 'Yeah, a bit,' I said.

'What about Shane? How well does he know her?'

He was looking straight at me and I had to concentrate hard to make sure my face never flinched.

'I don't think anybody has that much to do with her really. She stays in her room most of the time, and she dun't say a lot when she comes out.' I put a bit of a puzzled look on then and said, 'Why?'

Donny reached forward and pushed a button on the dashboard; my seat started to heat up straightaway. He tapped his cigarette against the edge of the ashtray, then said, 'She's a Kaler.'

Now I had to make sure I did flinch. I tried not to overdo it, but I took a quick breath in and made my eyes get wider. 'No way? We didn't know that.'

'No, I've only just found out myself.' Donny twisted round in his seat a bit and rested his elbow against the car door. 'But you see the person that told me, also said that young Shane's been screwin' around with her for months.'

Jesus. A sharp bit of metal cut into my thumb as I gripped the keys even harder. I went for what I hoped was a surprised but doubtful expression, and I shook my head as well. 'Nah, she's not his type – way too shy. He's never even said anythin' about her to me, and I think I'd know if he were – I mean I do live there.'

I was saying anything. I didn't know if I was making it better or worse, but lying, to Donny, about something like that; believe me, it weren't easy.

'So you think my friend's got it wrong then?'

I blinked. The cigarette was quivering in front of me, and I pushed my hand further down on to my knee to try and keep it steady. 'Well, I'm not with him twenty four hours a day, am I? But I'm pretty sure there's nothin' goin' on between 'em'.

Donny stared at the fag I was holding, before he looked up at my face again. I tried to smile, but the hot trickle of sweat running down the inside of my arm made it hard.

Nothing moved or made a sound for what seemed like about half an hour, but it was probably only a minute. I was desperate for another drag, but I couldn't trust myself to get the fag to my mouth without shaking.

A few seconds later, Donny reached round and put his seat belt back on. 'OK. That's sound then,' he said.

My mouth fell open just slightly as I relaxed.

'You can see why I had to check it out though, can't you?' He turned the key in the ignition. 'I mean, I'd need to know if it were true; it's important. But you said you're sure about it, so that'll do.'

Donny put the radio on, then drove me back to Chapel Cross without saying another word.

Just as I was about to get out of the car though, he turned to me. 'It's been good talkin' to you, Mikey,' he said. 'But I'd appreciate it if you could keep our little chat to yourself, alright?'

'Sure,' I nodded, and as I shut the car door behind me, I breathed properly for the first time since he'd picked me up.

I walked around for ages wondering what to do. I

knew I had to tell Shane that Donny was on to him; I knew I had to have another go at getting him to dump Jasmine. But I'd already taken a big risk by feeding Donny a load of crap. If he found out I'd gone running back to Shane chattin' about something he'd asked me to keep quiet, I'd be in as much shit as anybody.

The other thing I wondered about, was where Donny'd got the information from. The freaky twins knew about Shane and Jasmine of course, but did they know who her family were? And if they did, who'd they blabbed to so it got back to Donny?

I thought about that night at Rocco's flat when I'd told him about Shane having a proper girlfriend. Had he found anything else out about her? And if he had, would he grass Shane up to Donny? I didn't think so, but I couldn't be sure.

It could even just be somebody who'd seen 'em together. Over the last few weeks Shane'd been more careful, but at the beginning he'd taken her out a lot; skating, films, meals – anybody could've seen 'em.

There was a good chance Donny hadn't even believed me as well – I mean, I'm hardly Will Smith when it comes to acting – he might already know I'd lied to him, and it might already be too late to do anything about it all.

Christ, what a mess.

But by the time I got back to the house, I'd made my mind up what I was gonna do. Shane wizz a mate, wasn't he? And he'd always looked out for me. So although it meant I probably needed my head looking at, I decided I was gonna tell him. I couldn't do anything straight away, just in case Donny had somebody watching us, but tomorrow, tomorrow I thought, I'll have one last go at trying to talk some sense into him.

***

I needed to get us somewhere well out of the way. I didn't want to talk at the home in case it was somebody from there who was snuggling up to Donny. So it had to be outside. Donny was gonna be away all day cos of the Manchester deal, so he was well out of the way, but I didn't feel like I could trust anybody anymore.

It was OK for me and Shane to be seen together – that was normal – but it had to be somewhere where there was definitely no chance of us being listened to. The best place I could come up with was the park. I sent Shane a text asking him to meet me there straightaway.

I got there first. It was a weekday and there weren't many people about, just a few old blokes walking dogs and a few young lasses pushing prams.

Shane turned up after a few minutes, and as there wasn't anybody else using it, we went into the kids' playground.

He sat down on one of the swings and looked up at me. 'So, go on then, what's the emergency?' He smiled.

I knew there was nobody anywhere near us, but I couldn't help glancing round again just to check.

Then I moved a bit closer to Shane and took a deep breath. 'Donny picked me up in his car last night,' I said. 'Took me to some industrial estate that was all deserted.'

He frowned. 'What did he want?'

'He asked me if I knew Jasmine. He told me about her bein' a Kaler,' I paused to take another breath. 'He wanted to know if it's true that you're … seein' her.'

Shane's head dropped down. He put his hand up over his eyes, then slowly moved it back and ran his fingers through his hair. 'So what did ya say?'

'I told him it was a load of shit. But he's on to you, mate, I swear down. I don't know who's told him but somebody has, and I'm not sure I managed to persuade him they'd got it wrong.'

'But you made out it weren't true; you said there was nowt between us, yeah?'

'Yeah, course I did.'

He looked back up at me. 'You're a proper mate, Mikey.'

I managed to smile, but not for long – now here comes the proper hard bit.

'So,' I said carefully. 'Now are you gonna call it a day with her?'

Shane looked away and shook his head slowly. 'I can't.'

'Yes, you can, and you'd betta do it now before he goes mental on you. Even if he already knows you've been with her, if you stop it now you can at least say you've only just found out; pretend you dumped her as soon as you knew. You could leave the home, move in with Rocco for a bit – that'd make it obvious you weren't seein' her anymore.'

'I can't. I've gotta be with her.'

'Why, for fuck's sake? I know she means a lot to you, but is she really worth two mashed up legs and a caved in face? You're actin' like a proper idiot. You know you could have any other bird you wanted within about five minutes of dumpin' her.'

He didn't say anything at first, and I wondered if I'd gone too far; if he was like proper mad at me.

But then his eyes moved back up to mine, and he said, 'She's pregnant.'

Jesus. I sat down on the swing next to him.

That'll do it alright. That really will be enough to completely piss everybody off. The Kalers'll go psycho. Shane, and Jasmine, will be in more trouble than any of us can even imagine. If she has it.

I felt really awkward saying it, but I needed to ask. 'Is she gonna keep it?'

He shrugged. 'Up to now, yeah. She's not exactly buzzin' about it, but she won't listen to me when I try to talk to her about not havin' it.' He paused to light a fag. 'What can I do? I can't force her into havin' an abortion if she dun't want one. I can't start tellin' her what to do now when it's my fault for bein' so stupid in the first place; I should've made sure it never happened.'

The swing moved gently as I pushed my trainers against the floor. I thought about it for a while, then took a bit of a risk. 'I know everythin's all messed up, but even if she wants to keep it, it still dun't mean you've got to stick around.'

He shook his head again. 'But I don't want it to be

like that, Mikey. All these years growin' up in kids' homes on my own, people only ever doin' stuff for me because they're paid to, because it's their job; not because they really care. All these years I've always thought I'd never let that happen to my kids. I'd make sure I was there; I'd look after 'em properly. You know, take 'em to school, kiss 'em goodnight, kick a ball about in the park? I can't just turn my back on 'em.'

There were some voices behind us then and we both spun round. But it was just a woman with a little kid in a pram. She came on to the playground and lifted him out, he was proper small and he looked like he'd only just learned to walk.

Shane stared at him. The kid made a babbling noise and toddled towards the swings where we were, then he stopped and pointed at the one Shane was sitting on.

'No,' said his mum gently. 'Come on, you can go on the green one today.'

She took his hand and tried to lead him off in the direction of one of the empty swings, but the kid started screaming and stamping his feet on the spot. 'Red one,' he yelled. 'Red one, red one, red one.'

Shane got up. 'It's OK. He can have it if he wants.'

'Oh, thank you, love,' said the woman, as she sat down on the swing, picked her baby up and put him on her knee. 'I don't know what it is with him at the minute, but everything's got to be red.'

Shane smiled at her, then he looked at the little boy again. He was laughing now, the kid; kicking his legs about as the swing went backwards and forwards.

After a couple of seconds, Shane turned away, and

we headed back towards the road.

'What now then?' I said.

'All I can think is that we'll have to get out of Sheffield – me and Jasmine. I'll have to tell her about Donny so she understands, then I'll get some money together and we'll go. I can't see any other way out.'

'I've got a few quid you can have, if it'll help?'

He nodded. 'Cheers, Mikey. You saved my life.'

I knew it was best for Shane and Jasmine to leave. I was almost jealous of 'em actually: going away, nobody knowing where, making a fresh start somewhere new; some place without Donny and without Kaler. Don't get me wrong, I was gonna miss him big time, but I was sure he was doing the right thing. And as long as I could convince everybody that I didn't know anything about it, everything else should carry on pretty much the same.

I started to cheer up. The more I thought about it, the more certain I was that within a few more days, everything would be alright again.

But then, Donny got shot.

EIGHTEEN

It was late the next morning when I finished reading the letter from Leon. It was proper good. He was talking about what we'd do when he got out again, and he'd even written those words I'd been waiting for: ... *if you like, you can come and stay with me and Chrissy?*

I wrote a letter back saying thanks and telling him I'd love to. Then I went straight out to post it, and it was just as I was putting it in the letter box, that Paulie came and stood next to me.

I looked at him.

'Alright, Mikey?' he said.

I nodded.

'I've come to give you a lift over to the caf.'

My heart started to thud so loud I could hear it. I looked round, wondering what to do. But what else could I do, really?

He took me round the corner to where Jake was waiting in a grey Ford Escort. Paulie got in the back next to me, then Jake set off. At first, I gazed out of the window and tried hard to look relaxed. But then I saw the freaky twins outside the chippy, and although he completely ignored 'em, they made a big deal about waving to Jake as we went past.

Christ, that wasn't good, was it? Trying to look relaxed suddenly became impossible.

When we got to the café, Tyler opened the door. I could see Rocco inside, but Shane wasn't; I wondered if he was on his way.

Donny was laid in the big leather chair and he was

breathing hard. His left arm was across his chest, and the top of it had a bandage wrapped round it.

'What's happened?' I said, and it was obvious I really was shocked.

Donny lifted his head up a bit and said, 'A bullet, Mikey, that's what's happened.'

He sounded calm, but his eyes made it clear that he wasn't; they looked like they'd iced over; it was as if there was nothing there behind 'em anymore.

'It was just off the Snake Pass,' he went on slowly. 'As I drove back from Manchester last night.'

'Are you OK?' I asked, realising I ought to sound concerned.

'Well, it could've been worse. They fired three. Only one hit me, and it didn't do much damage. I managed to drive away.'

I stood there in silence, not knowing what to say next, or even if I should say anything at all.

After a bit, Paulie looked at me. 'We know who did it though,' he said. 'In case you're wondering.'

'Oh, who?' I asked.

'That Kaler bastard. He actually went out there himself with some of his boys – they didn't even try to cover it up.'

Donny got out of the chair and paced round the room. 'Yeah, and I'll take care of him soon. But the really important question though, I mean what I keep askin' myself, Mikey, is how did they know I was gonna be on that road at that time? You see because of what happened before with Rocco, I'd kept it proper quiet. Only people that I completely trusted knew about it; like the boys.'

My insides twisted and my mouth dried up. Slowly, I began to realise what he was getting at, and I knew then that Shane wasn't gonna be invited to this little meeting.

I kept my face blank and didn't say anything.

Donny glared at me, then carried on. 'So, it's got to be one of us. And I'm thinkin' who? Which one of my boys has a reason to sell out to Kaler? And then I remember somethin'; I remember what somebody told me about Shane and that Kaler lass. And I make some more enquiries, and I find out it's all true.'

My head dropped as he came over and put his hand on my shoulder. I knew I should've probably looked back up at him, but I couldn't make my eyes move – in fact, I don't think I could've made anything move.

'But you told me there weren't anythin' goin' on with 'em, didn't you, Mikey?' He stopped talking and waited for me to answer, but all I could manage was a bit of a nod. 'Well, I'm gonna give you the benefit of the doubt. I'm gonna believe you didn't know anythin', and that you didn't do anythin' wrong.'

He squeezed my arm, then leaned in closer. 'Shane though, he knew everythin'. He knew it was some dirty little Kaler slag he was shaggin' all along. And Kaler must've got to him – one way or another – so he set me up.'

I shook my head, but I still couldn't look at him. The first thing I felt were his hands grabbing my jacket, then a pain thudded through my head as he rammed me back against the wall. When he yanked my face up so it was

178

level with his, my heart felt like it was gonna bust its way right out of my chest.

'Don't even start tryin' to say I've got it wrong, idiot. I'm warnin' you, don't make me anymore mad than I already am.'

My eyes were down but I could feel him watching me. I stopped breathing completely.

'Shane's messed up,' he went on. 'And now he's gonna pay for it.'

He let go of my top and I thought I was gonna cry, right there in front of 'em all. My head was spinning, but I knew what I needed to do; I needed to get out as soon as I could and warn Shane. They had to get away, now, today.

But Donny was cleverer than that.

He laughed. 'I know he's your mate, Mikey; I know you're already thinkin' about tellin' him. But you're not gonna do that. Firstly because, well, let's face it, you're not really gonna get the chance. But also, cos of your brother.'

My head snapped up and I stared at him. 'What d'you mean?' I whispered.

'I mean, he's a sittin' duck in Dalton. You know I've got friends in there – good lads they are, loyal, do anythin' for a mate – 'specially if it involves slicin' somebody up. They're already waitin' for me to give 'em the word.'

My legs started to go from under me then.

Donny flicked his head at Tyler who was sitting just to my right, and Tyler got up.

'Sit down,' Donny said to me.

I had to, or I would've hit the ground.

'So, you're not gonna say anythin' to our Shane cos you want to keep your brother alive. What you are gonna do, is you're gonna bring him to us. We've been watchin' that home all mornin', and he hasn't set foot outside it yet – maybe he knows somethin's wrong? But you're his best mate, he trusts you, and in half an hour's time you're gonna make sure he's at Frankie's.'

It felt like the room was caving in on me. All I wanted to do was get out, but everything was crushing me down; everything was holding me where I was. What was I gonna do? How could I keep 'em both safe?

Donny watched me, before he brought his hand up and slowly ruffled my hair. 'There's nothin' you can do except what I've told you to do, Mikey. Anythin' happens to you, or me, or any of the other boys, and the next time you see your Leon he'll be laid in the bottom of a box.'

He ran his hand down the front of my coat 'til he felt the knife in my inside pocket. 'And I'll look after this for a bit as well.' He took it out, turned around, but carried on talking as he walked away. 'Frankie's, at half-past one – you can phone him from here, then we'll all go round to meet him together.'

It was then that my mouth filled up with vomit. I put my hand straight up to my face and tried to keep my mouth shut, but I couldn't, and I felt it running out between my fingers. I bolted for the backdoor, not really expecting my legs to get me there, but they did, and just as I pushed it open, I threw up everywhere.

I was bent double as mouthful after mouthful of hot,

rour, yellow liquid just kept on coming up. My eyes watered and my throat burned.

Even when there was nothing left inside me to fetch up, my stomach retched and retched. I coughed, gasping for breath, black flecks flashed about in front of my eyes. I was choking, I thought I was gonna go down.

But my shoulder hit the wall then, and kept me more or less upright. A second later I managed to suck in a big gobful of air. I straighten up and wiped my mouth on my jacket. Gazing round, I saw Paulie standing in the doorway watching me.

'Get back in here,' he said.

I concentrated hard to put one foot in front of the other, and I made it inside.

Donny glanced at the clock on the wall as I shuffled past. 'Phone him now,' he said. 'And be convincin'.'

I reached into my jeans' pocket and took my phone out.

I was still frantically trying to come up with an idea, any idea; but what could I do that'd work? He'd got it all covered.

If I didn't do it, Shane might get away. But it wasn't definite. Donny'd already decided he'd set him up for Kaler to shoot at, and even if this didn't come off, he'd still try and get him some other way, I knew he would.

And, if I didn't do it, they'd kill me. Believe me, I'm really not trying to sound like some kind of a hero here, cos I'm not. But actually that would've been fine; it would've been so much easier than having to make that call.

But it was Leon, wasn't it? It was Leon who'd held me tight, who'd started to care about me … who'd said he wanted me to live with him.

I didn't want him to die.

I blinked as I looked down at my phone. I tried to press the right bits of the screen to unlock it, but my whole hand was shaking. Paulie snatched it off me and sighed. When he handed it back, it was already ringing.

Shane was buzzin' when he answered it. 'Hey, Mikey. You alright, mate?' he said.

'Yeah …' My voice sounded like it was miles away.

'Listen, we're gonna go later today. I've told Jasmine why and she's sweet about it. I'm just sortin' the last few things out. I wouldn't have been able to do it without that cash ya gave me.'

I looked round the room; all the other boys were watching me. 'Can I buy you some dinner?' I said.

'Nah, you're alright. Will you call back in though, so I can see ya before we leave?'

My throat tightened. Donny got up and moved closer until his mouth was a few inches away from my ear. 'C Wing,' he whispered.

And the words just blurted out on their own. 'Please. Just meet me at Frankie's, about half one.'

'OK, I'll be there. But what's up?'

I was struggling and starting to cry again. Donny took the phone off me and ended the call.

'Is he gonna be there?' he said.

I nodded, blinking to try and stop the tears.

'Wicked,' he smiled.

And my heart stung like it'd been slashed open with

182

a broken aftershave bottle.

Wicked. Yeah, that's what it was. But not wicked like he meant, wicked like it always used to mean: nasty, vile, selfish. That's what everybody'd think about me now, wouldn't they? That I'd turned into some proper, evil, cold-hearted bastard. And perhaps they'd be right.

But it wasn't their brother.

Anyway, it's all pretty hazy and blurred after that. We waited a few minutes, and I think Jake went to sort the car out. Paulie gave me a different coat and a balaclava and told me to put 'em on.

I remember looking at Rocco before we left, and just for a second, the heaviness in my stomach lifted; maybe there was something he could do? Rocco's face showed the tiniest sign that he understood, then he put his head down.

Donny glanced between us. 'Tyler, you stay here with Rocco, will you?'

The heaviness came back, and it was worse than ever.

I'd got Paulie on one side and Donny on the other as we walked into Frankie's, and they were both holding guns. There was a guy waiting to be served, but he must've decided he wasn't as hungry as he thought, and he left without buying anything.

Frankie took one look at Donny and disappeared into the back.

I stood there between 'em, shivering and shaking and hoping he wouldn't come; just go I thought, for God's sake, just get yourself out of it all.

A stabbing pain cut into my chest as a dark figure appeared on the outside of the frosted window. But it carried on past, thank God. I stared at the door. The next time it opens, Shane'll probably walk through it.

I pictured it all. Shane walking in with a grin on his face. His eyes bright; full of hope for the future he was gonna share with Jasmine. After a split second though, he'd realise. He'd realise what I'd done to him and his eyes'd grow big and scared. He'd look at me, not believing it could be true. But then there'd be a shattering blast as Donny pulled the trigger. Shane's body'd smash back into the doorframe, slide down slowly into a heap on the floor. Straightaway, blood'd spread all around him – and it'd be red, and gushing, and a mess; just like on that film. Then, as it soaked up into his jeans and hoodie, his face would glare up at me; pale, and young, and lost.

I couldn't let it happen; I just couldn't.

Very, very carefully, I leaned my head slightly forward. Donny's gun was down by his side. My fingers trembled. Steadily, I started to move my hand towards it.

But I froze as an image of Leon's smiling face hurtled into my head. It was like I could feel his arms around me again, like I could hear his words and his laugh. But then he got pulled away. A vision of Donny's mates took over. They surrounded him. Leon's eyes flashed as a silver blade carved through his stomach, he fell towards me, went down hard. The floor became an ocean of blood; my brother's blood. And then, as huge tears rolled down her face, I imagined

Chrissy, standing there staring at me.

Thoughts flashed in my head like fireworks. They were too quick for me though; I couldn't concentrate on any of 'em. My dripping wet T-shirt clung to my back and the ice-cold sweat made me shudder. I reached up, yanking at the neck of my coat; it needed to be loser, I needed to breathe. The floor tilted and I rocked; almost passing out, but Donny gripped my arm even tighter.

Somebody's voice managed to cut through then. I blinked, trying to get my mind to sort itself out.

'He's late,' Paulie said.

Donny took his phone out to check the time. Without really thinking, I glanced over at it.

'Only a few minutes,' Donny said. 'He'll be here.'

I've no idea what time it said on the phone, cos as all the other stuff in my head gradually cleared, the photo on the screen held my gaze. It was of Donny with his arm round this lass, and I'd seen her before. I couldn't remember where, but there was something about her, something important that I needed to get. My brain went crazy trying to work it out.

She wasn't from round here, I was sure of that. Not from any of the clubs or pubs. I'd not noticed her with any of the boys. So where? Where'd I seen her that meant she'd stick in my memory?

It took two or three more seconds, then I gasped. 'It's her,' I said, looking up at Donny.

'Eh?' He seemed more surprised that I'd dared to say anything at all, rather than at what I'd actually said.

Paulie's nails dug deep into my other arm. I hesitated, but forced myself to go on. 'That lass, on your phone … did she know you were goin' to Manchester yesterday?'

The phone clattered to the floor as he reached out and dragged me up to him. 'What you tryin' to say, you little shit?' He had a handful of my coat in one hand, and his gun in the other.

I opened my mouth but nothing came out. I glanced up over his shoulder and looked at the door again; for God's sake, get on with it, I told myself.

'She came out of Kaler's house,' I managed. 'That night, just before we hit 'em. She kissed one of their boys before she went.'

Donny's eyes flickered, then went back to being cold and hard.

'You're lyin',' he said, and even though he was so close to me, I was straining like mad to hear him. 'I know you are, cos Paulie's seen her loads of times; he'd have recognised her.' He took his eyes off me for a second and looked across. 'Wouldn't you?'

Paulie stroked his chin. 'Sure.'

I frowned. How the hell could he have forgotten? More to the point, what the hell could I do to make him remember? I scrambled back in my mind to that night, trying like crazy to think of all the details. 'The Mini.' My eyes lit up. 'She got into a yellow Mini, didn't she? Drove it away?'

Paulie stuck his bottom lip out and shrugged like he had no idea what I was talking about. I couldn't believe it; why was he doing that?

Donny's dark eyebrows dipped though. 'Dun't mean a thing,' he murmured. 'So what if she did; it's not like there's only one yellow Mini in the world, is it?'

'No, but that's her; definitely. It's the truth.'

'It's bullshit. You'd say anythin' to get your mate off. Now shut it before you piss me off proper.'

'But ...' I shook my head as much as I could with him still holding my jacket. 'It is her, I swear down –'

'Shut your fucking mouth!' Donny's hand sprung up. I flinched as the cold, solid barrel of the gun hit the underneath of my chin and stayed there. Every breath he took sent a long, warm, rush of air along the side of my cheek. I tried to shy away, but the more I leaned my head back, the harder he dug the barrel into my skin.

I closed my eyes. This was it. Without even noticing it, my thoughts turned into desperate, high-pitched words. 'But you must remember, Paulie. That necklace, that diamante thing – you talked about it when we got back to the house ...'

The air on my face suddenly stopped being warm. The grip on my coat slackened. Slowly, I opened my eyes; Donny's silent gaze burned right into me.

'What diamante thing?' Paulie bent down to scoop Donny's phone up off the floor and examine the photo. 'Now we know you're makin' it up; there in't even no 'S' on this necklace.'

Donny's whole body jerked.

He blinked. Then nothing; absolute stillness, absolute quiet.

My shoulder blades pressed back against the wall tiles. The air I took in nearly stretched my lungs to bursting.

Releasing his grip on me, Donny turned to Paulie.

'You knew,' he said.

Paulie licked his bottom lip but didn't answer.

'You did see her at Kaler's house.'

'No.'

'You must've done.' The hand with the gun in it dropped down a bit. 'That's how you knew about the 'S' on her necklace, the necklace she wore before I bought her that new one ... and, before I ever introduced her to you ...' Donny backed off towards the door. His head shook and his mouth fell open. 'I trusted you ... you were my mate.' He sniffed as his face screwed up. 'And I trusted her ...' Then in the loudest voice I'd ever heard him use, he cried, 'Shona!'

His hand went to his forehead and he stumbled slightly. Paulie took a quick step forward, but immediately Donny's gun flew back up.

'He's lyin.' Paulie threw me a look that made me freeze. 'I haven't done owt; I just guessed at the 'S' cos of her name. It's Shane what set you up.'

Donny's eyes darted between us. The barrel of the gun followed 'em. My spine went rigid.

And at that second, Shane walked in.

Donny whizzed round. The bang threw me right back against the wall. Automatically, my eyes closed and my arms shot up to cover my face. I struggled to keep my balance and reached out to try and steady myself. Eventually, my hand grasped the edge of the counter and I got myself back up straight, then I forced my eyes open and held my breath.

Paulie was pointing his gun out in front of him, Donny's body was sprawled in the doorway, and Shane was standing behind it looking stunned.

My head fell forward as I breathed out. All I could do was stand there, trying hard to take it all in.

But Paulie didn't hang about. 'Get his gun,' he yelled, as he pushed Donny's phone into his pocket.

I stared at him. He had known, hadn't he? Known all along that the new girlfriend was passing information back to Kaler. Known they'd be setting Donny up first chance they got.

He glanced at me. 'Just get the gun,' he said, but this time his voice was quieter.

I bent down ever so carefully. The skin where the bullet'd come out of his back was all split open, the flesh around it mashed up, and the bright red spots splattered across the floor. I swallowed hard. They'd been right about all that; it was just like they'd said.

But that was as far as any watermelon similarity went.

Because Donny had eyes, and they were still wide open; blue and clear and glaring. A stream of blood tricked out of his mouth, the colour'd drained from his face – I knew he was dead, it was obvious. But those eyes; those eyes watched me all the time, and they made my hand shake so much as I leaned over, I could hardly take hold of the gun.

'Move it, will ya?' Paulie shoved me towards the door, forcing me to step over Donny's body. I glanced at Shane, but Paulie pushed past me and spoke to him first. 'I don't wanna see your face round here no more,' he said. Then to me, 'I'll see you, back at the café.' He spun round, almost knocked an old guy flying, and raced off towards the corner where Jake was waiting in the car.

Me and Shane stared at each other. I could tell he was working it all out; putting everything together. Any time now he was gonna get it. Then what?

Some woman nearby was screaming into her phone. 'Ambulance, Ambulance,' she yelled.

I knew I had to be quick, but what could I say?

Shane looked round, then back at me. 'I'll phone ya, Mikey, yeah?'

I know it's really crap, but all I could do was nod, and after standing there for a couple more seconds, we turned away and headed off in different directions.

NINETEEN

All I looked at for the next few weeks was the inside of my bedroom at Holly House. I almost threw up if anybody tried to see or talk to me, and even the smell of food made me feel like I was choking. I just laid there, wrapped in my duvet, and thought.

Somehow, despite Paulie's lies, Donny's temper and me being useless, Shane had lived. He'd got away, and him and Jasmine'd gone off somewhere together – just as planned.

But that was only because of luck and coincidence, right?

If I hadn't seen that lass that night, if Donny'd been wearing a watch instead of having to get his phone out, if I hadn't remembered who she was in time …

Well, then Shane would have been dead.

And although Paulie knew about that Kaler lass all along, and knew it was probably her who'd betrayed Donny and not Shane, none of that really mattered, cos it didn't alter the fact that I'd set my best mate up to be murdered, and it was only luck and coincidence that'd saved him.

So easily, it could have been Shane who ended up with a bullet through his heart, and Donny who walked away.

How could I have done it? How could I have phoned him up, conned him into coming to Frankie's, then stood there doing nothing while they waited to kill him?

A dull pain hung under my ribs constantly.

I didn't know where they'd gone to, Shane and

Jasmine. I had no idea if they were safe, and I didn't know what he thought about me anymore. He'd said he'd phone, but would he, really, once he'd had time to take in what I'd done to him? And, if he did, what would he say?

Twice, I worked my way up to phoning him, but both times it just rang and rang and rang. Maybe he didn't have the phone anymore? Maybe he was ignoring me? I hoped to God it was cos of the first reason.

Another thing I thought about a lot, was Donny. I kept expecting to hear *Not Afraid* on my phone, and for him to start telling me what he was gonna do to us all when he got his hands on us. Although thinking about him laid in that doorway made me shudder, I had to keep on doing it, cos it was the only way I could convince myself he really was dead.

Somebody who didn't need convincing about Donny being dead though, was Paulie. The only calls I could face answering were from Rocco. We never talked about what'd happened at Frankie's, but he told me Paulie'd started running S16, and that he was loving it.

Cos that's what he'd been after all along; I could see it now. Jeez, his face must've lit up like Blackpool illuminations when he'd first seen 'em together. And if things'd worked out how he thought they would, S16 would've dropped into his grubby little hand without him even breaking into a sweat.

That Shona girl did her stuff alright: got Donny hooked, found out what she needed to know, fed back to Kaler. Kaler even got a bullet in. But it wasn't enough.

So when it came down to it – when I recognised her and Paulie made the biggest slip up of his life – as well as stabbing Donny in the back, Paulie also had to shoot him in the chest.

I saw it all over and over again, thought the same thoughts, felt the same guilt. Sometimes I managed to fall asleep, but never for more than a couple of hours at a time, and even then, the mess in my head wouldn't leave me alone.

So when my phone rang late one night, I was still awake but fairly spaced out. Cos I hadn't been answering it for so long, most people'd stopped trying to call me. I picked it up slowly and looked at the screen. The number was a new one that I didn't recognise. I was gonna turn it off, but for some reason, I pressed the button and waited for them to talk first.

'Mikey?'

'Shane! Mate, is that you?' I was so buzzin' to hear his voice, I forgot about everything else for a second.

'Yeah, it's me. You alright?'

Am I alright? I'm better than I ever thought I'd be again. I stood up. 'I'm sound. What about you? Where are you?'

'Some crap place near the sea. It were alright at first, but now it's doin' my head in – nothin' happens, like ever. I think we're gonna move again soon, ya know, back to one of the cities? Apart from owt else, I've gotta start earnin' again.'

'But you're OK, you and Jasmine?'

'Yeah, yeah, we're good. I'll tell ya what though, I

never knew being pregnant made ya throw up so much. Owt starts her off; I can't even have a fag in the house, and the other night I had to stand outside in the rain to eat my curry.'

We laughed, then it went quiet for a few seconds. I walked over to the window – I had to say something, didn't I? My mouth opened, but Shane spoke again.

'So …' he said, much quieter. 'What's been happenin' round there?'

My voice sounded funny cos I was short of breath. 'Oh, Paulie's havin' a right birthday; apparently he's walkin' about like he's some proper big time drug baron or somethin'.'

Shane laughed again, but I was too busy thinking about what I needed to say next.

I bit my lip and squeezed the phone hard. 'That day, at Frankie's … I … '

'Mikey, it's OK. I talked to Rocco; he told me about it.'

'Did he?'

'Yeah – everythin'.'

'What … and you mean you still …'

'I mean, it's cool. I know ya didn't have a choice … I'd have done the same.'

'But – '

'Mikey, forget it. If it weren't OK I wouldn't be phonin' ya, would I?'

My grip on the phone loosened, and I smiled. He was letting me off. He was still my mate; he didn't hate me.

'What happened though,' Shane asked. 'I mean how

come Paulie ended up blastin' Donny?'

I told him about the photo and everything.

When I'd finished, he said, 'You did well to recognise her, mate, I don't think I would've done.'

'It were when she walked past me,' I said. 'The streetlight was right on her; she just stuck in my head.'

'Well, cheers for tellin' him. It must've took some guts. I bet Paulie coulda battered ya!'

We both sniggered a bit, then there was another pause before Shane said, 'Have the cops been talkin' to ya?'

'Nah – not yet, anyway. Accordin' to Rocco, they think it were Kaler's boys who hit Donny, and that it were Donny who killed that kid outside their house. It makes sense I suppose, and so far, it's keepin' 'em off our backs.'

'Cool. What about us? Are they lookin' for Jasmine?'

'You were reported missin', I heard Ruth tellin' somebody on the phone when you first went. I don't know anythin' else though; I haven't been out much.'

'How come?'

I put my head down and didn't answer.

'Have ya seen anythin' of ya brother?'

'I haven't even talked to him.'

Shane didn't say anything, but I knew he'd be wondering why I hadn't been in touch with Leon. Before he had to ask, I added quietly, 'I've been proper messed up ...'

Jasmine's voice sounded in the background, shouting Shane's name.

'I'll try an' come over to see ya,' he said to me.

'Don't be daft.' My voice suddenly got loud. 'You heard what Paulie said.' I meant it as well, as much as it would've been wicked to see him, I wasn't going through all that again.

'You've gotta get yourself sorted though, mate.'

'I will; it'll be better now.'

Jasmine shouted him again.

'OK. Listen, Jasmine wants me, I'd betta go. You can get me on this number now though; anytime, yeah?'

'Yeah, course.'

'See ya later?'

'Yeah, later,' I said, and we hung up.

I flopped back down into bed, shut my eyes and started to laugh. Shane was OK about it all. He was still my mate, and him and Jasmine were safe. All at once everything seemed easier. I laid there just enjoying that feeling, but not for too long though, because within about half an hour, I was bang out.

***

The next day I woke up early. My eyes were wide open and my mind was buzzin'. I got up, got dressed, and decided I wasn't gonna rely on luck and coincidence anymore.

First, I phoned Chrissy.

'Oh, I was beginning to think you'd left the country,' she said when she heard my voice.

'Yeah, sorry. I ... How's Leon?'

'He's OK. He's been worried about you though; we

both have.'

I couldn't talk to her about it, I just couldn't. 'So, what's been happening with Social Services?' I asked her.

'Well I only got through to speak to somebody yesterday, but they said the assessments are almost complete. Apparently, they'll have a decision really soon.'

'D'you think it'll go our way?'

'I don't know, love. But I can't see why not.'

'Thanks, Chrissy,' I said, and if I could've reached out and hugged her, I would've done.

Next, I went down to the office to talk to Ruth.

'Will you phone school?' I asked her.

'What for?' she said, flicking through the diary.

'I ... I wanna see if I can still do some exams.'

'Bloody hell!' She didn't quite fall off the chair, or drop the diary, or faint; but it was a close thing. 'I'll do it now. You're making a really good choice, Mikey. There's still some time left before you leave, I'm sure they'll be able to help you settle back in and catch up on what you've missed.'

'I don't wanna go back,' I said. 'I just want you to find out if I can take the actual exams.'

She snatched the phone up with one hand and looked the number up with the other. I listened until I knew they were saying yes, and then I went out.

OK then; so that was two bits of my life more or less sorted. The other thing I needed to do though, was a million times harder.

Paulie was on his own at the café when I got there. It

was the first time I'd seen him since that day, and I decided to stick to what I'd gone there for, and not even go near any of the other stuff.

'You took your time,' he said, stretching out on the leather chair. 'I'll get ya some gear sorted.'

Obviously, he'd had the same thought.

'I don't know if I can,' I said quickly, before he had chance to get up. 'It's Social Services – they're takin' more of an interest since Shane went. They're checkin' what time I get in; asking loads of question, wanting to know where I've been – and, who I've been with.'

Paulie's small, cagey eyes held me still. I tried my best to look cool, but I knew if he saw through the lie he'd go psycho on me.

He wasn't convinced at first, I could tell. I'd seen him murder Donny and I knew Jake'd killed that Kaler kid. If he decided I was backing off just cos I wanted to, if he didn't buy the Social Services thing, he'd put two and two together and come up with grass.

'I'll carry on if you think it'll be OK,' I said, shrugging. 'I just thought I oughta let you know.'

He stared at me for a bit longer, then sighed. 'Alright – keep your head down for a bit, but just 'til things cool down.'

'Sound,' I said, and I tried to get out before he could say anything else, but I couldn't.

'Be careful who ya talk to though, Mikey, won't ya? I mean, Social Services might not be the only ones watchin' ya.'

I nodded, and went.

***

As the following weeks and months went by, things just about stayed OK. Social Services agreed that I could go with Chrissy to see Leon, and that if it went well they'd, 'move towards increased contact' when he got out. Chrissy'd sounded as excited as I was when she told me, and we were just waiting to find out when the visit was gonna be.

School'd started sending somebody round to Holly House every Monday to do work with me and help me get ready for the exams. She was alright, the tutor, and I even did the extra revision stuff she left for me.

So, the only thing that still bugged me, was Paulie. Although he'd left me alone at first, I was certain it wouldn't last, and I was right.

One night when I was on BBC Bitesize, he phoned me. I hadn't the slightest idea what else I could say to put him off, and there was no way he'd fall for the Social Services stuff again, so I let it go to voicemail. I thought I'd got away with it when he didn't leave a message, but then a few minutes later, he sent a text instead.

All it said was, *fone me*. But those two words were enough to make me more nervous than a cat at Crufts. What if all the things that were going right suddenly got messed up cos of him? Getting picked up by the cops now, would mean everything else would have to wait – or maybe, never happen at all.

I worried about it right through the night, and all through the next day. And then, when Rocco turned up at the house wanting me to go with him, I was convinced my time'd run out.

'It's OK,' he said, as we got to the bottom of the steps. 'It'll only take a minute; I just need to tell ya summat.'

We almost walked past Frankie's, but at the last minute I couldn't do it, and we turned towards the park instead. When we were well away from anybody else, Rocco said, 'Paulie and Jake got busted.'

'You're kiddin'?' I stopped and gawped at him.

'I'm not. Five o'clock this mornin', the cops raided both houses. Paulie's bird says they've been charged with loads of stuff. It looks like they're gonna get remanded.'

'Do you think they know anything about us?

'Doubt it – they'd have got everybody at the same time if they did.'

Re-sult! I smiled at Rocco.

'I thought you'd wanna know,' he said.

My smile spread even wider.

'Anyway, I'm gonna take off. Look after yourself, yeah?'

I watched him walk away, then I set off back towards the home.

Yes; that was it. Now I could finally get away from 'em. There was nothing stopping me – unless they sunk proper low and grassed the rest of us up that is – but they wouldn't do that.

The cops must've had plenty on 'em to be keeping 'em banged up, and even if they got off with it all in the end, hopefully, they'd be inside long enough for me to get away.

I walked round for quite a bit then – it was cool being out and not having to bother about meeting up with Paulie or Jake. So it was probably about half an hour later when I got a message alert on my phone.

Me and Shane'd been talking to each other every few days, so I wasn't surprised to see it was from him. I was gobsmacked though, when I looked at it and saw the picture he'd sent. It was of Jasmine, gazing down at a tiny, dark haired baby all snuggled up in her arms. The words he'd written just said, *my daughter*.

I stopped and leaned back against a wall. So she'd come early then; there's no wonder she looked so little. But everything must be OK or he would've said.

The baby's eyes were all sparkly and wide open, and she was looking right into the camera. One of her hands was gripping the edge of her blanket, and I couldn't believe the size of her fingernails; they were like grains of rice or something.

It was good that Shane and Jasmine were both there for her, wasn't it? She deserved that.

After a bit, I sent a text back and put my phone away.

So that was it then. Shane'd got the girl – well, he'd got two of 'em actually. The bad guys'd got what they deserved. And me? Well, in a few weeks' time, Leon'll be out and I'll be moving in with him and Chrissy; I'll get my family.

I smiled as I stood up straight and set off walking again; all we need now, I thought, is for us all to live happily ever after ...

It'd got a whole lot darker while I'd been standing there. The street behind me was all in shadows and everywhere I looked was deserted.

But by the time I turned the corner on to the road where Holly House was, my phone was buzzing with another message, and the streetlights were just flickering on.

Also by Kate Hanney

SOMEONE DIFFERENT

Two very different backgrounds; two young people who need each other.

When teenagers Jay and Anna are thrown together unexpectedly, their secret love ignites.

But when his world of neglect and youth crime collides with her parents' high expectations for her education and show-jumping success, that love has to battle to stay alive. Will their deep feelings and desperate sacrifices be enough to keep them together, when everything else is pulling them apart?

SOMEONE DIFFERENT is a story of how teenage love struggles to survive when the realities of parents, friendships, prejudice and deprivation get firmly in its way. Set against the contrasting backdrops of an inner-city housing estate and an idyllic country estate, the book takes its readers on a dramatic, compelling and sometimes violent journey, in which the characters' only defence against all of this, is each other.

SAFE

The Book For Teenagers Who Don't Read

Isolation at school, rows at home, spending a night in the cells - Danny's used to that kind of trouble; that's normal.

But then he hits on a posh girl at a party, and life at home goes from bad to worse. And after that it's not just normal trouble anymore.

And it's not just Danny who's in Danger.

Lightning Source UK Ltd.
Milton Keynes UK
UKOW04f1805190315

248182UK00001B/5/P